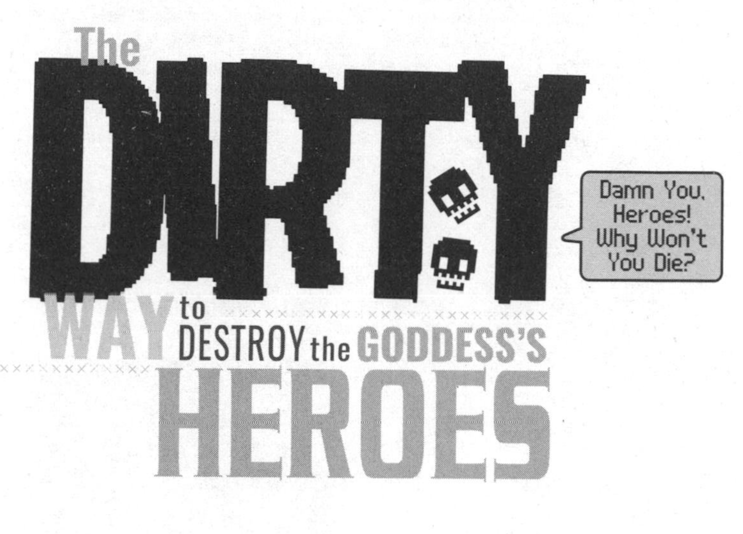

1

SAKUMA SASAKI

Illustration by **ASAGI TOSAKA**

New York

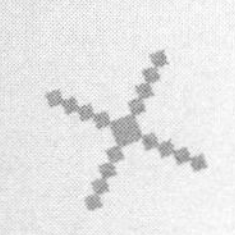

The Dirty Way to Destroy the Goddess's Heroes
Sakuma Sasaki

Translation by Jordan Taylor
Cover art by Asagi Tosaka

First published in Japan in 2017 by KADOKAWA CORPORATION, Tokyo.
English translation rights arranged with KADOKAWA CORPORATION, Tokyo through TUTTLE-MORI AGENCY, INC., Tokyo.

Yen On
150 West 30th Street, 19th Floor
New York, NY 10001

Visit us at yenpress.com
facebook.com/yenpress
twitter.com/yenpress
yenpress.tumblr.com
instagram.com/yenpress

First Yen On Edition: July 2019

Yen On is an imprint of Yen Press, LLC.
The Yen On name and logo are trademarks of Yen Press, LLC.

Library of Congress Cataloging-in-Publication Data
Names: Sasaki, Sakuma (Novelist), author. | Tosaka, Asagi, illustrator. | Taylor, Jordan (Translator), translator.
Title: Oh, heroes! they just won't die / Sakuma Sasaki ; illustration by Asagi Tosaka ; translation by Jordan Taylor.
Other titles: Oo yusha yo! shinanai towa uttoshii. English
Description: New York, NY : Yen On, 2019. | Series: The dirty way to destroy the goddess's heroes ; Volume 1
Identifiers: LCCN 2019011081 | ISBN 9781975357115 (pbk.)
Classification: LCC PL875.5.A76 O613 2019 | DDC 895.63/6—dc23
LC record available at https://lccn.loc.gov/2019011081

ISBNs: 978-1-9753-5711-5 (paperback)
978-1-9753-5712-2 (ebook)

10 9 8 7 6 5 4 3 2 1

LSC-C

Printed in the United States of America

The DIRTY WAY to DESTROY the GODDESS'S HEROES

Damn You, Heroes! Why Won't You Die?

contents

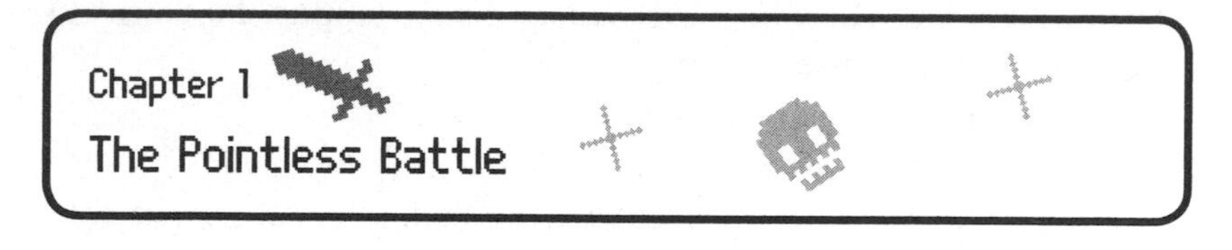

He suddenly realized he didn't know where he was.

But Shinichi Sotoyama wasn't easily shaken by strange events. He was seventeen years old and in his second year of high school, where he wasn't an active member of any clubs. He did well in the sciences and just okay in the humanities. He was perfectly average.

Well, that wasn't entirely true: He was average in all things, except his courage. Unlike most people, he could always keep his composure. In fact, when a car hit him in the fourth grade, Shinichi didn't seem bothered at all by his broken left arm. Onlookers screamed and shouted, but he just calmly pulled out his cell phone with his right hand to call for the police and an ambulance.

Justifiably exasperated, his father had asked him, "You've got a few screws loose, don't you?"

Here was his latest predicament: He'd been riding the train, only to teleport (the only probable explanation) to some fantastical place. He now stood in a massive hall carved from stone, with a magic circle drawn on the floor.

But Shinichi had taken this absurd phenomenon in stride.

There's no way something like a manga would happen in real life, right?

Now, however, he had on an uncharacteristically cold expression, and unlike his usual cool self, he was sweating bullets.

"...!"

He was so focused on keeping himself from shaking, he forgot to blink. He just stared straight ahead.

A colossal figure towered over him.

Shinichi quickly estimated the brute was over ten feet tall, twice his own height, with arms and legs thicker than tree trunks. His core muscles wrapped around his body like the armor of a tank, and as if to cockily suggest any actual armor was unnecessary, he wore only a loincloth and cloak. All this gave the imposing specimen the appearance of some ancient Spartan warrior or the physical manifestation of raw, furious force.

Facing each other, they must have looked like a kindergartner squaring off with a sumo champion or an elementary school student being attacked by a grizzly bear.

That alone would've been plenty to give Shinichi pause, but the strangeness didn't stop there. This behemoth of a man had deep blue skin and two massive horns sprouting from his head. He was clearly some kind of monster—and most definitely not human.

There was absolutely no way Shinichi could defeat him.

On top of it all, the displaced high schooler was terrified to the very core of his being by an invisible force around him.

"Hmm..."

As if to examine something, the giant bent down toward Shinichi. The air around Shinichi trembled before pounding into him, wave after wave, as if in a storm at sea. It might've been the aftershock of the creature's magical or supernatural powers, and Shinichi realized this monstrous, massive man wasn't simply a beast of incredible physical strength: He was a weapon of mass destruction in humanoid form, a collection of massive energy, overwhelming his surroundings in one short breath.

There's just no way. I'm just as good as dead.

There was nothing he could do. He'd clearly never been in a fight before and was obviously at a disadvantage in terms of strength, so combat was out of the question. If he turned his back to escape, this monster would surely pounce on top of him.

All Shinichi could do was sigh, knowing his life was over.

Huh, dying at seventeen. Well, I guess it wasn't a bad life, but I kind of wish I wasn't dying a virgin.

Shinichi was too scared to beg for his life. Instead, he began wondering what the giant thought of him—just standing there, trembling, silent, and staring back.

Menacingly, the gargantuan figure slowly walked up to him and swung his trunk-like arms for his finishing move...

Then he groveled so violently in front of Shinichi that the ground rumbled.

"Please save us, young man!" pleaded the giant with ardent desperation.

"Uh...what?" replied Shinichi.

"Please! I can grant you anything your heart desires! Please use your wisdom to do something!"

"Um? Uh?"

"Those disgusting humans keep taking advantage of my daughter's kindness—!"

"Wait! Calm down!" shouted Shinichi.

The monster's angry howls blasted out of his open mouth like a typhoon, forcing Shinichi to cling to the ground to prevent himself from being blown away.

"Oh, how often I've considered just slaughtering them all! Wait! It's not too late—"

"Daddy, please calm down." A bell-like voice rang out behind the titan's epic stature just as Shinichi's hands were about to give.

Instantly, the wind died down. The air stood so still it was hard to believe it had blown with such intensity a moment before. It was the same with the creature's face: It was no longer contorted in rage and softened to let out a smile overflowing with joy.

"Oh, my beloved Rino! You're still just as dazzling as the blue sun!" exclaimed the giant.

A young girl peeked out from behind him. She looked only about ten years old, though she wore an exquisite, extravagant dress. Everything about her was enchanting: Her hair was a lustrous jet black, her skin as white as snow, her eyes the color of rubies. In fact, she was so bewitching, Shinichi found himself staring at her, even though he had no predisposition toward little girls.

"Daddy, this isn't the time for that," she said to the behemoth (who was apparently her father, despite bearing no resemblance). He held her closely in a big bear hug, cradling her small body against his cheek.

She pushed him away.

"What…? Do you hate your daddy?!" The monster reacted in shock, but the girl didn't seem to notice—or care. She walked up to Shinichi and delicately gathered her skirts to make an elegant curtsy.

"I'm glad to make your acquaintance. My name is Rinoladell Krolow Petrara, but please call me Rino," she said.

"It's a pleasure to meet you. My name is Shinichi Sotoyama: first name, Shinichi, last name, Sotoyama."

"Shinichi… That sounds a little weird. You really must be from another world…," remarked Rino, mulling it over. She smiled sweetly at him, charming him for a moment, but her father radiated such a murderous rage that he hurriedly put together a stern expression.

"So this really isn't Earth?" he asked.

"I don't know where this Earth is, but this world is called Obum," she clarified.

"And you used some sort of magic to summon me here?"

"Yup, that's right! Daddy hoped you'd be able to help us," explained the girl, nodding as she answered his questions. She turned back to her father. "Daddy, it's rude if you don't introduce yourself."

"…You bastard, ignoring me while you ingratiate yourself with my daughter! I swear, I'm going to incinerate you, burn you to ashes…," growled the giant.

"Daddy! I really don't like it when people can't even introduce themselves!"

"Yes! Welcome, wise one from another world! I am the great and terrible Blue Demon King, Ludabite Krolow Semah!" he boomed, delivering his name with regal pride and pomposity. The grand reveal fell a little flat, though, seeing as he only did it to avoid upsetting his daughter.

"…Thank you, Demon King. I am Shinichi Sotoyama," said Shinichi, doing his best to give a stiff reply. He was no longer afraid of imminent death. He was more disturbed by the strange situation in front of him.

The Demon King nodded in satisfaction at Shinichi's deeply bowed head.

"Would you look at that! The boy knows his manners. He's pretty sharp, too. You're completely different from the previous pathetic, filth-spewing insect."

"Previous?" asked Shinichi without thinking.

"Yes," answered Rino with a pained look on her face. "You're actually the second person we summoned from another world. The first wasn't, well, quite as calm as you are..."

"He wet himself the moment he saw me, started sobbing, shouted meaningless drivel, writhed and wriggled all on his own, and then died," interjected the Demon King.

The poor thing probably had a heart attack. One look at the Demon King could certainly have that effect. All things considered, it wasn't surprising that's how it ended.

"That person— No, you know what? Never mind," Shinichi said. He was going to ask what happened to the corpse. When he realized they might say they feasted off his body so it wouldn't go to waste, he got flustered and shut his mouth.

Rino seemed to read Shinichi's thoughts and started to explain. "Shinichi, please don't misunderstand. The first boy—"

"Pardon the interruption, Your Highness, Lady Rino." As the massive door creaked open, a voice intruded. A single maid with dark brown skin and silver hair walked in. Her ears were long and pointed, resembling those of a dark elf, but she was undoubtedly drop-dead gorgeous.

"...Celestia, what is it?" The Demon King was impatient, but sensed he needed to deal with an urgent matter.

Under the King's visibly vexed stare, the maid calmly reported, "*They* are here again."

"Again, those disgusting maggots, graah!" he shouted, letting out an earsplitting bark. A scorching blast of air whipped around, heated by the King's fury. "I'm done with them! I've called upon the wise one for this, but it was all in vain, as I will use my own hands to kill them—"

"Daddy! Please calm down! Please don't do anything awful!" Rino cried in an attempt to soothe her enraged father. She tried wrapping her arms around one of his legs, but it was too thick. As she held on to him, though, the bloodthirsty rage flickered from his eyes, and he tenderly stroked his daughter's hair.

"You're right. I'm the most fortunate man in the demon world to have the most wonderful child in the world, my beloved Rino."

"And I'm so glad to be the daughter of such a kind daddy," she responded sweetly.

The Demon King chuckled. "Oh, don't flatter me like that! Daddy just might get so excited he blows away the red sun!"

"……"

Shinichi was bored by their excessive display of affection, but the maid seemed used to their interactions and called out to the King.

"Your Highness, I regret to disturb such a beautiful moment, but you must be on your way to the southern lands."

"Oh, of course. I'll make those maggots pay for ruining this tender exchange between father and child!" he said as he placed an unimaginably massive hand on Shinichi's shoulder. "Perfect timing. If you would be so kind as to accompany me, I shall show you the reason why I summoned you."

"What? What's that sup—," Shinichi tried to say, but a disorienting, floating sensation overwhelmed him from speaking any further. Before he could blink, they moved from the great hall to a grass field squeezed between some mountains.

"Did we teleport? Amazing…," said Shinichi. Having come into this world using teleportation, he felt a little silly commenting on it now, but he couldn't help himself. He was awestruck by these magical phenomena.

He would soon realize he didn't have much time to soak it all in.

"Scorching flames ignite! *Fireball!*"

Just as Shinichi heard a woman's voice call out in the distance, his ears started ringing from the sound of an explosion.

"Wha…?"

His field of vision suddenly filled with a flash of crimson light, followed by the sensation of hot winds, carrying the nauseating smell of burned flesh and making him want to vomit.

A feeling of dread filled him, but he reflexively looked toward the source.

"Is that…a minotaur?"

He saw the bull-headed humanoid standing a few hundred feet from them. The minotaur seemed to have sustained damage from the explosion. His entire body was burned raw and red, and white smoke rose from his body as he collapsed onto the ground.

"I—I can still fight, *moo…!*" The bull-headed beast attempted to stand. It was a mystery how he still lived despite his injuries.

But before he could get on his feet, a blade swung down and callously severed his head from his body.

"Dammit, that one was stubborn," cursed a man clad entirely in full plate mail as blood dripped from his sword. He had the appearance of a human knight. Behind him, Shinichi could see there was a male warrior wielding an ax, a male ranger carrying a bow, a priestess swinging a mace, and a sorceress holding a twisted wand.

"These are…," Shinichi began.

"These are the maggots who have laid waste to my people," the Demon King spitefully finished before disappearing from Shinichi's side and reappearing in front of the knight and his party.

"You come again and again and refuse to give up, you maggots. I assume you're prepared for what's to come."

"Ah, let's go everyone!" the knight called. For a brief moment, he seemed to show fear under the Demon King's death glare but immediately regained his composure.

The five attacked at once.

"*Slicing Gale Blade!* Hyah!"

"*Destruction Ax!*"

"*Three-Shot Burst!*"

"Divine Goddess, grant me an iron hammer of justice against evil! *Force!*"

"Scorching flames ignite! *Fireball!*"

For a moment, the Demon King's body disappeared beneath the rapid movement of slashing swords, swinging axes, three arrows, an invisible force, and a sphere of flames deployed by the battle party.

"Yeah! We got him!" A satisfied grin appeared on the knight's face, as he was certain there was no way the Demon King could've sustained all those powerful attacks and still be standing.

But from his position, Shinichi could see otherwise. The knight spoke too soon. To the almighty King, their attacks were as ineffective as a mosquito bite.

"Is that all?" he boomed as the flames began clearing. The smoke blew away to reveal his face, with an expression far surpassing anger, and his completely uninjured body. "And to think you actually had me… Begone, pathetic pests!" He raised his right hand, closed into a fist as if to crush an apple.

In that moment, the ranger's body twisted and burst into pieces.

"Gaah…!"

His blood, sinew, and brain tissue sprayed out in a disgustingly dazzling display of fireworks. Shinichi grimaced at the sight, but the Demon King's enemies didn't seem shaken by their companion's death at all.

"Press your attacks! Don't let him use his magic!"

"Hyah!" roared the warrior next as he swung his ax at the colossal figure and finally landed a hit. But to the Demon King, the attack was as gentle as a baby's hand reaching up to slap him in the face. After all, his body was pure muscle, further reinforced with an inordinate amount of magical power.

"That doesn't even itch," he said smugly as the ax deflected off his muscular chest. He balled both of his hands together, slamming them onto the fighter's head.

The warrior's substantial six-and-a-half-foot frame flattened to the thickness of a plank.

"Ha-ha-ha, is this a cartoon…?" Shinichi was so beyond horrified at this excessive display of violence that he could only laugh. Far away, the knight's party refused to run, continuing to launch attacks at the Demon King.

"Don't falter! Charge!"

"Hyah! *Force!*"

"Fireball!"

"...Maggots." Apathetic, the Demon King didn't attempt to dodge their moves.

The party was full of one-trick ponies using the same attacks. He entertained them a bit by withstanding all of them, then swung his right hand up to activate his first spell of the battle.

"Flames that flicker in the heart of the world, remove this filth! *Blue Raging Flare!*"

Hotter than red flames, more luminous than white, blue hellfire erupted from the ground. It was so bright it almost blinded Shinichi and indiscriminately scorched the entire battlefield.

"Are you *trying* to kill me?" shouted Shinichi. Though he stood far away, the air was hot enough to burn his skin, and he readied himself for death again.

A wall of light suddenly appeared in front of him, blocking the scorching gale.

"A barrier...?" he whispered in wonder.

"They really are a foolish lot," the dark-skinned, silver-haired maid remarked sharply, standing beside Shinichi, who was stiff from fear.

"Uh, Celestia, right?" he asked.

"You may call me Celes, Lord Shinichi," she replied.

"Oh, okay. Thank you for saving me, Celes," said Shinichi, hesitantly expressing his gratitude and extending his hand. Celes glared at it suspiciously.

"What do you think you're doing? Do you intend to grope my ass and use that memory to pleasure yourself later? Disgusting," she spat.

"It's disgusting you'd assume that!" Shinichi protested before realizing the misunderstanding.

Is it not customary to shake hands here? Well, I guess we're in a different world. I mean, she's not even human.

Shinichi retracted his hand, conscious yet again that he was in a completely foreign world. With that, the slaughter—it'd be wrong to call it a "battle"—was over, and the Demon King returned to the two, looking just a little triumphant.

"Celestia, I leave the rest to you. I'll be returning to the castle."

"Understood, Your Highness." Celes bowed deeply before advancing into the field, circumventing the land that had melted into glass under the extreme heat.

Shinichi was finally composed enough to look around. He noticed a number of corpses scattered across the field: The knight's party had killed more than just the bull-headed beast from before.

"So this is what a battle is like..."

Kill or be killed.

There was no justice nor morals. The strongest was the one left standing. The only rule was survival of the fittest. As he realized this, Shinichi felt neither fear nor revulsion. Perhaps it was because the reality of the situation had yet to hit him. He still couldn't process being summoned to another world or seeing the King's absurdly overabundant display of power.

And yet, five strangers were now dead. That was the only certainty he knew.

The Demon King let out a bored huff when he saw Shinichi's concerned expression.

"Humph, calling this a 'battle' is an affront to the name of the Blue Demon King. Playtime's over," he grumbled.

"That was play for you...?"

If this behemoth fully unleashed his power, the ground would certainly break into two, and the sky would surely tear. It might even look like those paintings of Judgment Day when all hell broke loose.

This was why Shinichi's question came up again.

"Why'd you summon me of all people?" he asked. He just couldn't figure out why this tremendously terrifying beast would need the help of a puny, little high schooler so badly he'd get down on his knees and beg.

But the Demon King simply waved Shinichi's query off.

"I'm tired today. We shall speak more tomorrow."

What he had in power, he certainly lacked in responsibility.

"Wow, and to think you're the King..."

"Silence! Today, I get to bathe with my daughter and read her a book before bedtime!"

"Wait, isn't that a crime?! Rino's too old for that! (I think?) Geez, cut the cord already!"

"Be quiet, be quiet! She always said she was 'gonna marry Daddy'! Yes, it's fine!"

"How many years ago was that?!" In the face of such unhealthy parental attachment, Shinichi forgot formality and lashed out at the Demon King with an impolite retort.

The Demon King didn't respond. Instead, he placed his hands on Shinichi's shoulders and activated his teleportation magic. In that split second, as they teleported off the blood-soaked battlefield, Shinichi suddenly felt like something was off.

Wait. Were two of the men's bodies missing?

The bodies of the first two killed—the ranger and the warrior—had disappeared from the battlefield. Shinichi wondered if they'd been obliterated by the blue flames, but he didn't dwell on it too much and quickly forgot all about it.

"Good morning, Lord Shinichi."

Most boys only dreamed of being woken up by a busty, tan, silver-haired beauty in a maid outfit, so Shinichi made sure to soak in this precious moment, even though he was feeling low.

"Well, I figured it wasn't a dream," Shinichi muttered, resigning himself to his fate and getting out of the extravagant bed in the guest room.

"Breakfast has been served. This way, please," said Celes, exiting the room with Shinichi scurrying behind her in tow.

His stomach growled.

Oh yeah, I guess I haven't eaten anything for, like, an entire day.

Shinichi had been so worn out by the events of the day before that he'd immediately fallen asleep once he'd been shown his room. Consequently, he still hadn't learned why he'd been summoned.

"This way," called Celes. She led him into a room, smaller than he anticipated for a dining hall in a castle. In fact, it was only about the size of a classroom, though the ceiling was fairly high to accommodate their ten-foot-tall monarch as he entered and exited. In the center of this chamber, the Demon King and Rino already occupied the middle seats of a marble table, which looked quite expensive, as they awaited Shinichi's arrival.

"Good morning, Shinichi," chirped Rino.

"Morning, Rino," he replied.

"First, we eat. Then we can talk," commanded the Demon King.

Celes pulled out a chair for him, and Shinichi accepted the monarch's offer to have some breakfast. But when Celes placed a plate in front of him, he couldn't help wrinkling his nose in disgust.

"What *is* this?" he exclaimed.

Gilded with gold accents, the plate looked inconceivably expensive, which brought even more attention to the purple…*thing* on it.

"*Parbegut* meat," answered Celes.

"Come again?"

"Like I said, it's a roasted *parbegut*."

"……" Though Celes took the time to expand on her original comment, Shinichi couldn't make sense of it and sat in stunned silence.

Up until this point, Shinichi had been conversing pretty normally with the Demon King and everyone else, but he hadn't, in fact, been speaking Japanese. Thanks to a magic spell that freely translated between the two languages, Shinichi had been speaking quite naturally in their tongue. This spell had probably been activated when he was summoned.

For example, just now, when Celes said "roasted," she'd actually pronounced it "*bibinana*." The spell took the word *bibinana*, translated it to "a dish of roasted meat," and simplified it into "roasted," just like our great teacher, Goo–le. And it did all this right inside Shinichi's head so he knew exactly what they were saying.

Though the spell worked astonishingly well, it didn't necessarily download their vocabulary into his brain. So if a word had no equivalent in Japanese, it was left as it was. In other words, the spell couldn't suggest a replacement for *parbegut*, the meat of some mysterious animal that definitely didn't exist on Earth.

"What's wrong? Are you not going to eat?" asked the Demon King, giving Shinichi a strange look while picking up the purple-colored flesh and setting on it voraciously.

Well, the meat probably wasn't poisonous—at least, that's what Shinichi wanted to believe. Then again, weren't onions poisonous to dogs but safe for humans? So this wasn't remotely a guarantee the dish was safe for him. Despite all this, he knew it'd be rude not to eat the food he'd been given.

And Shinichi was starving.

He gathered every last bit of courage, picked up the *parbegut* meat with his hands, and closed his eyes as he bit into it.

"...That...is *vile*." After chewing ten times and swallowing, that was the only way he could describe the experience. "Seriously, what the hell *is* this?! It's absolutely disgusting!"

Though aware this was expressly not how a guest should respond to a feast, he couldn't stop himself. This mysterious *parbegut* was so repulsive, even his hunger—the world's best spice—did nothing to mask its taste.

Its texture was squishy like clay, and a raw fishy odor emanated from its juices. The fat had neither the sweetness nor the bitterness one might expect from meat and tasted exactly like nothing. It was so disgusting it made him question his entire existence. He would've much rather eaten paper instead. And couldn't he get a little bit of praise and recognition for keeping it down rather than vomiting it back up?

"Something must be wrong with the ingredients if this thing tastes so terrible roasted. Roasting something is, like, the simplest way to cook... Or are my taste buds weird?" he asked, suddenly self-conscious. It could very well have been that this was considered gourmet in this world. Maybe their palates were different from his.

If that was the case, he felt bad for his outburst and sheepishly looked at the Demon King, who shook his head grimly.

"You're not in the wrong. This is part of the reason why I summoned you."

"What?" Shinichi gaped, incredulous.

"It isn't just *parbegut*. Even to us, all foods from the demon world are, um… very not good," explained Rino after hesitating for a moment. Her sweet smile was replaced with an uncharacteristic bitterness.

"I know not why. All I know is all food from the demon world is absolutely foul," said the Demon King.

"Okay, could you please explain everything to me—starting with this 'demon world'?" asked Shinichi. Obviously, this world of darkness—this demon world—had to exist, since they had a Demon King, but he didn't want there to be any misunderstandings.

"Well then, allow me to start," offered Celes from behind, responding to Shinichi's question. "Intelligent creatures born with magical prowess are who we call demons, and the world in which we reside is called the demon world."

"Uh-huh…"

"Unlike the 'human world' and its rising red sun, the blue sun always shines in the demon world. There's no such thing as night," she continued.

"A blue sun? I'd like to see that sometime," said Shinichi. Though it certainly piqued his interest, he realized it probably wasn't entirely safe. He'd probably die instantly of suffocation under their poisonous atmosphere.

"Anyway, as Lady Rino explained, the food available in the demon world is all unpalatable," continued Celes, getting the conversation back on track.

"Though most people don't seem to mind and keep eating it…," said Rino. Her face was sad as she recalled the time no one listened to her talk about the importance of taste.

"Have demons lost some of their taste buds due to the environment?" inquired Shinichi.

The number of taste buds—the receptors on your tongue that sense flavor—vary among animals. For example, herbivores have lots of taste buds to avoid eating poisonous plants, while carnivores have very few as they simply eat the spoils of the hunt. There were even animals, like snakes, that had no taste buds at all.

"Maybe," he speculated, "in exchange for your taste buds, your stomach evolved into one that's strong as steel and resistant to food poisoning or something."

"I wonder. I do believe those resistant to poison have dulled tastes." Celes cocked her head as she considered Shinichi's theory.

Regardless, the majority of demons weren't at all concerned with taste. On the other side, there was the minority, like their ruler and his daughter, who were aware of the terrible flavors but had endured them up until now...or something like that.

"Mommy loves to travel. She's visited all kinds of places. A little while ago, she visited the human world," said Rino.

"She left 'to find someone stronger' than her. Unfortunately, though, no human was strong enough to satisfy her," the Demon King added casually.

"What are you, some kind of martial arts group?" quipped Shinichi dryly. This information made it an even greater mystery how the Demon King and his equally combative wife had raised their daughter to be such a good and honest child.

"When Mommy came back, she brought me food called bread from the human world."

She'd given leftover human food to her wide-eyed daughter upon returning home. This gift had carried no deeper meaning. After all, her mother was generally uninterested in flavors and didn't place much value on human food. Her daughter, however, reacted theatrically after placing the bread in her mouth.

"It was just so delicious...," recalled Rino with a smile melting across her face.

Later, Shinichi would discover this bread was more like hardtack—heavily salted and dried out to prevent it from spoiling. Born in twenty-first-century Japan with its tasty treats, Shinichi would've found it barely edible, calling it too hard, too salty, and too disgusting. In fact, if he were to rate it on a scale from zero to one hundred, it

would've scored a solid five. But compared to the food in the demon world, which would've scored negative one thousand, it was so delicious to Rino and her sensitive, young palate, it could've opened heaven's gate to paradise.

"Ever since then, I can't stand to eat our food...," confessed Rino in a sad whisper.

"And I could no longer bear to watch my daughter wither away, so I decided to enter the human world in search of good food!" boasted the King.

"I can't believe you invaded the human world just for that...," said Shinichi.

Though weary of the King's alarming attachment to his daughter, he could sympathize with their decision, remembering Rino's crestfallen face and their soul-crushingly unpalatable food. Given *parbegut* meat was being served to this world's supreme ruler and his darling little daughter, it must've been the highest-quality food available. Even still, it was undeniably stomach churning. This was more than enough reason to invade the human world. In fact, wars were waged over black tea in human history, so Shinichi really wasn't in a position to criticize.

Just as Shinichi felt he was starting to get a grip on things, the Demon King resumed his speech.

"Don't misunderstand my intentions," he warned. "Yes, I came to the human world and built a castle, but I have no intention of slaughtering the humans to take their food."

"Uh, really?" asked Shinichi in surprise.

"Yes, I told Daddy I'd hate for him to do something so cruel," added Rino with a happy smile.

"It'd be so much easier just to destroy those maggots...," grumbled the Demon King discontentedly.

"Daddy!"

The Demon King coughed to cover his remark and continued.

"Anyway, because of my gentle daughter's sweet mercy, I chose this deserted mountain range as our base."

"I see," said Shinichi, who decided to take his word—for now.

He thought back to the battle the day before. They all fought in a narrow valley closed off by mountains. It was true it didn't seem particularly suitable for farming, good for raising livestock, or even easily accessible. It's not surprising it'd been abandoned, and it wouldn't have been profitable to develop such infertile land anyway.

"And yet, the humans sent their army without a declaration of war, even though we'd done nothing to them!" shouted the Demon King in a rage.

"Yeah, well, I also get their point of view, too…," said Shinichi, sympathizing with the humans.

Even though the lands were wild and served no use, the humans had come face-to-face with strange monsters suddenly appearing near their country. Hell, this area might have even been in their territory. Left alone, these creatures could certainly have invaded their lands, and the humans decided to make the first move to prevent this from happening. It wasn't a terrible decision, really.

But they did miscalculate one thing: Their enemy was the almighty Demon King. They had no hopes of defeating him. (Not that he had a desire to harm them to begin with.) They really should've first sent out a scouting party to evaluate the entire situation.

"Though they only deployed six thousand soldiers, they caught us off guard and killed many of my loyal followers, who came along seeking better flavors."

"……"

"I was enraged, of course, and killed half of them outright, driving the rest away."

"…Well, I also understand why you might act that way," said Shinichi.

If you try to kill someone, it's only expected they'll try to kill you back. It didn't matter if you're in another world. This was the rule. It always held true.

Rino became flustered when she saw Shinichi's pained expression and tried to explain further.

"Please don't be sad, Shinichi. No one died."

"Huh? But he just said he killed half of them…" Shinichi was troubled by this blatant contradiction, but he didn't have time to think about it any further.

The door to the dining hall suddenly swung open.

"Your Highness, we have a problem, *moo*!" came a voice.

"What the—?"

As the figure approached, Shinichi rubbed his eyes, unable to believe the sight in front of him: A sturdy body was crowned by a bull's head, the same one that'd fallen to the ground the day before.

"Kalbi, it looks like your body is doing well already," said the Demon King.

"Yes, thanks to Celes, *moo*," he replied.

Upon hearing the King's concerned tone and looking at the beast's flexed biceps, Shinichi decided he wasn't just a look-alike.

"Is this a joke...?"

He wasn't talking about the twisted humor behind naming the minotaur Kalbi. He was talking about how Kalbi's head had been cut off, how he'd been undeniably dead and yet was standing here in front of them, which meant—

"But more important than that, Your Highness, they've returned, *moo*!"

"...Of course," said the Demon King, bored half to death by this completely expected turn of events. He stood from his chair and placed his giant hand on Shinichi's shoulder once again.

"Let us depart," he commanded.

"......"

Shinichi said nothing in response. He just kept imagining the nightmare that awaited them once they teleported to their destination.

"The Demon King's here!" roared the armored knight, brandishing his sword. The warrior, ranger, priestess, and sorceress responded to his battle cry, drawing their weapons.

It was like they'd all gone back in time. The day before, they'd been reduced to nothing—yet, here they were, standing in the same field in the same exact way.

"What the…?" Shinichi recoiled, but he'd already started to understand the situation. All the while, he was overcome with a familiar sensation of spine-tingling fear.

This time, though, it wasn't because he was afraid of the Demon King.

"To think they'd casually have a spell for resurrections in this world…," he muttered.

The dead came back to life.

This obviously would've been impossible on Earth, where death was irreversible. But this world had the miracle of magic, just like a video game. But if death could be reversed, what problems would they face? Shinichi understood this concept intellectually, but his brain couldn't process his surroundings. The knight and his party continued attacking the Demon King in the distance.

"Today's the day we take your head! *Slicing Ga—*"

"Land Bite." Instead of letting the knight finish, the Demon King cast a powerful spell right off the bat.

A mass of stony teeth erupted from the earth, skewering the party and immediately destroying them.

"Damn them all," grumbled the Demon King as he walked to the corpse of a pig-faced orc, killed at the hands of the party.

"Wake from your eternal sleep. *Resurrection.*" As the King chanted this short spell, a mystical light enveloped the corpse. In an instant, the cuts on his skin started to vanish, his heart began beating again, and the light returned to his unfocused eyes.

"Uugh… Your Highness? Oh no, I've inconvenienced you again, haven't I? That's unacceptable, *oink*," he said.

"Pay no mind. More importantly, round up those who are uninjured and bring the fallen to the castle. Celestia's ready to begin resurrecting them," instructed the Demon King.

"Understood, *oink*!" acknowledged the orc as he dashed off toward the castle, a little unsteady on his feet. After all, he'd just come back to life a moment before.

"You're rigging the game, bringing the dead back to life," said Shinichi, still surprised by the scene. It threatened to reverse his understanding of the nature of the world.

But for some reason, the King's face became clouded when he heard Shinichi muttering softly.

"If anyone's cheating, it's them! Look!" he said, pointing at the skewered bodies of their enemies. He indicated the mysterious light suddenly surrounding the cadavers and taking them from the scene.

"Their corpses disappeared… Did they teleport somewhere?!" asked Shinichi.

"I know not what trick they use. I've attempted to prevent this by leaving no trace of their bodies, like I did yesterday. But they still come back! You can't possibly expect me to let this go!"

Shinichi made a guess based on the Demon King's indignation.

"So normally, someone can't respawn without a body?" he asked.

"Exactly! The *Resurrection* spell is more effective the less damaged the body is, so if there's any less than half a head, it's impossible," replied the King.

Up until this point, Shinichi had assumed anything was possible in the demon world, but as it turned out, their magic had some limits.

"And that's why I left the bodies of those despicable human soldiers intact! Yes, I might've killed them. But I was considerate enough to leave half of them alive so they could carry the corpses to someone capable of resurrecting them, and yet…!" ruminated the King bitterly.

"I see. So that's why Rino said no one died," remarked Shinichi.

In other words, they could all be brought back to life. Since no one was dead, they technically shouldn't have anything to complain about. Obviously, thc knight and his party—and by extension, the humans—were capable of resurrection. The difference was they could somehow resurrect missing corpses, which was big news, because the Demon King was considered the most powerful being in this world.

Does this mean there's someone more powerful than him?

If that were the case, they'd be powerful enough to take on the Demon King. But that hadn't happened yet.

Let's see… I wonder where they come back to life. Maybe in a church or something… In a game, you kind of expect to respawn, so I guess I'd never given it much thought.

At first glance, this place was like a fantasy video game, but it wasn't actually a collection of electronic signals. It was a real world with living, breathing creatures, made of flesh and blood. And the demon world had its own rules and systems in place, even though they went against his earthbound knowledge and common sense. So no matter how much Shinichi thought about it, he was no closer to an answer. He simply didn't have enough information.

"Now then, Shinichi. As your summoner, I shall give you your task," said the Demon King pridefully, in a voice appropriate for his royal title. "Do something about the humans who keep coming back to life!" he announced forcefully, entirely unsuited to the wishy-washy nature of his pathetic command.

In response, Shinichi gave an exasperated retort. "*Do* something? I'm weak and puny! I mean, I can't even use magic."

"I have no expectations for your strength, but I'm asking you to lend me your wisdom!" boomed the King.

"Hmm..." Shinichi stroked his chin as he thought.

"What? You're not thinking about refusing, right? We spent such a long time casting the spell to summon the wise one. Oh, come on. At the very least, you must have enough wisdom to save us," begged the Demon King desperately.

"I'm flattered, but are you sure the spell worked?" asked Shinichi.

He had no doubts about the Demon King's magical strength, but if he needed someone with great wisdom, Shinichi was sure there were far better options than a student like himself...

"No, it was successful. You're unafraid to speak to me as an equal. That's more than enough proof. Sure, the first insect we summoned was intelligent, but he had no courage. But you're not so cowardly. And unlike him, you weren't quick to die without cause," he bellowed reassuringly.

"Okay, so that's why it had to be me."

Plenty of people were more intelligent than Shinichi, but not many had enough screws loose to casually chat with the almighty Demon King.

I guess this was a one-in-a-million chance.

Whether he was lucky or unlucky was up to him to decide.

"Okay, before I give you an answer, I've got a question of my own: What happened to the first guy?" asked Shinichi.

"My daughter began sobbing and begging me to resurrect him, so I gave in and sent him back to his world," revealed the Demon King.

"Which means there's a way for me to return to Earth. And what happens if I say no?"

"My daughter's not here now to stop me… You get what I'm trying to say, right?" The Demon King peered into Shinichi's face with a sinister smile.

The angelic Rino may act as his moral compass, but the Demon King was still peerlessly powerful, ruthless, and egotistical.

"So you're basically eliminating all other choices…" Shinichi cradled his head in his hands and let out a sigh.

But he already knew the reason he was chosen among the seven billion humans on Earth. He was fairly intelligent, he had that damned courage, he didn't yield to those with absolute power, and—

*Coming up with an all-out plan to defeat the indestructible humans who've confounded even the Demon King sounds…like…*fun.

A smile so sinister it could rival the King's spread across his face. He had a foul and dirty personality, finding joy in creating underhanded strategies to defeat his enemies, interested in plans that disregarded morals and social standards. This part of him had been latent, useless in the abnormal peacefulness and safety of twenty-first-century Japan.

It'd be such a waste to throw away a fun opportunity for fear of death. I mean, we're just all socialized to believe life shouldn't be wasted.

Back in Japan, he could only unleash his true nature in video games, but here, he could use it as much as he liked. He might go an entire lifetime without this kind of satisfaction again.

Shinichi was gambling with his life and the chance to return to Earth, but this was a price he was willing to pay. There were very few fools who'd be willing to sacrifice their lives, which was exactly why Shinichi was summoned.

"Understood, Your Highness," confirmed Shinichi, finally addressing the King formally, as he knelt in front of him to declare his choice: "With these hands, I will definitely defeat these death-defying 'heroes.'"

This was the moment a traitor was born: the Dirty Advisor of the Demon King's army who chose to fight against his own kind.

Chapter 2

Humans Need Their Souls (lol)

In a place a two-day walk southwest from the Demon King's castle, there was a flat landmass with a large flowing river, bountiful fields of crops that spread throughout, and a fortified city surrounded by stone walls.

This was Boar Kingdom. They'd sent six thousand soldiers against the Demon King and lost half their army. Rumors about the monsters—the legendary demons—spread throughout the country, accompanied with stories of the army's defeat. Dread crept up on the faces of the townspeople, fearing the demons would descend on the city at any moment.

There was one group of people, however, sharing drinks at the tavern, making a cheerful racket. It was as if they'd never heard of the word *fear.*

"Whew, that was another spectacular death," shouted one man, the ranger, shaking with laughter.

"We didn't do anything, though," insisted the sorceress, stunning as always. "But I suppose that's to be expected with an enemy like that."

"...Mhm." The male knight wordlessly agreed with them both.

"It's still a little disappointing," said the priestess, quiet and reserved, and the leader of the group, the knight, nodded deeply in agreement.

"It is. But we'll win in the end," he maintained without any arrogance or pretention in his voice. Though he said this with confidence, they still hadn't managed to leave a single scratch on the Demon King who'd killed them again.

But continuously challenging this undefeatable enemy was part of their plan.

"Okay, yeah, he's strong. But if we keep attacking him, his magical powers will eventually run out if he keeps firing off those powerful spells."

This magical power was necessary to cast spells. Even if one used up their supply, the resource replenished once you rested and recuperated. Recovery time, however, wasn't necessarily fast, correlating with the person's maximum magical capacity. For example, magicians' apprentices might be able to completely regain their powers within a day, but sorceresses, priestesses, and other first-class magicians would need at least two. This applied to the feared Demon King, as well. And though their actions were like trying to drain a lake one cupful at a time, the party knew there would be an end to the limited supply eventually.

"Which is why we leave the bodies of the small fry intact, right?" asked the ranger, a cruel smile twisting the corners of his mouth.

As long as they didn't burn the corpses and left them intact, the Demon King would use his magic to resurrect them over and over again. At first glance, this plan might seem foolish, but they were draining the Demon King's powers bit by bit.

"I almost feel bad that all his people are weaklings," professed the sorceress, purring with laughter, knowing that the orcs and goblins could be easily defeated with her magic.

She didn't feel a single shred of guilt for taking their lives. After all, she and her companions were on the side of justice, and the demons were evil filth defiling this world.

"Hey, hey, don't lose focus because they're weak. I mean, other than the Demon King," warned the knight in a joking tone, knowing they'd never lose and always manage to come back to life.

"We're the heroes of the Divine Goddess. We must fight gracefully to uphold the honor bestowed by this title," the knight grandly proclaimed.

His comrades raised their pints of beer in agreement.

"So their strategy is to wear the King down," observed Shinichi as he hesitantly chowed down on the mystery meat in the castle's dining hall. He saw through their strategy and reckless daily attacks upon listening to Celes explain magical powers and spells.

"Your Highness, let's just say they continue to attack like this. How many more days would your powers last?" he asked.

"I mean, they'd last for a year or two," the King replied.

"Wait, I thought that recovery time was slow...?"

Shinichi wondered why he even bothered to listen to Celes's lengthy exposition. The King huffed in annoyance at his confusion.

"Hmph, I am the Blue Demon King! Do not dare lump me in with those average plebeians! If I'm only using magic a few times to teleport and resurrect, I can recover it all in the course of a single night."

"I understand," said Shinichi, feeling like something was amiss and burying these suspicions deep in his heart.

"If I may be permitted to add, Your Highness is the only one capable of such high-speed recovery. The recovery time for your average demon is only slightly faster than humans," remarked Celes. Her face was as expressionless as it had been the day before, but her tanned complexion had taken on a pale tinge. Maybe it was for taking on the responsibility of resurrecting many of those who'd died, in order to lessen the burden on the King.

"What if you called all the strongest fighters from the demon world here to help?" suggested Shinichi, thinking that might lighten the load on Celes. "I mean, they obviously don't have to be as powerful as the King. But if they're strong enough to fend off the heroes' attacks, a guard of a couple dozen could reduce the number of casualties. Then the humans might realize their attacks are futile and maybe even give up," he continued with some optimism.

It was a good suggestion, but the King's and Rino's faces became grim as they listened to Shinichi.

"You're not wrong, Shinichi, but the powerful demons tend to be quite violent...," replied Rino.

"They'd ignore Rino's request and kill all the humans. You really can't trust that bloodthirsty lot!" yelled the King. He continued rebuking his subjects, though everyone else in the room knew the King was the most hotheaded of them all.

That explains why the demons here are all super-weak.

Though they had intimidating appearances, these demons were continuously defeated by the heroes due to their weak and timid natures. That said, they were still monsters who could kill an average person like Shinichi in one critical hit.

"So reinforcements aren't an option. But I have a feeling you'll be okay if you have inexhaustible magical powers—," began Shinichi.

"But I'm well on my way to the end of my patience," interrupted the Demon King.

"Ah..." The sight of the veins throbbing in her father's blue forehead prompted Rino to look down apologetically.

It was true that kindness was one of her virtues, making her want to prevent unnecessary causalities, even those outside her own kin. At the same time, these demands tied the King's hands, allowing the humans to make a fool of him and creating their current predicament. Taking things to the extreme, if the King were allowed to exterminate all of humankind, he'd probably be able to get rid of whatever trickery kept reviving the heroes and defeating them, as well.

Understanding this, Rino suggested repentantly:

"Daddy, if I stop complaining about the food being gross, can we just give up and go back to the demon world?"

"What're you saying?! I'd fight for a thousand years for my little girl!"

"I know you would, Daddy. But if it keeps going on like this, Mr. Kalbi or Mr. Sirloin will be killed for real..."

They'd been lucky so far, but if their bodies vanished without a trace, the foot soldiers could face death at any time.

"In that case, I suppose I must destroy all of humankind," insisted the King, itching to fight. He refused to sacrifice his people any longer, and this would be the fastest way to resolve their issue.

"But—but that...," stammered Rino, unable to find the words to persuade her father and looking around her for help. Her eyes met those of the silver-tongued Shinichi.

"Hmm, I can't say no to the requests of a beautiful girl," he said.

"What did you just say, you pervert?"

Shinichi shrank back in response to Celes's outburst and stood.

"I understand your frustration, Your Highness, but it'd be a waste to destroy humankind. Please reconsider your course of action," he advised.

"A waste?" asked the King.

"Yes. You ventured out to find good food, right? Well, the humans know how to cultivate and cook all that food. It'd be a waste to kill them."

"Hmm." The King found himself nodding in agreement to his logic. "But we have you. Isn't that enough?"

"I'm human, but I'm also from another world. Sure, I can cook a little bit, but I have no idea what the best food source is or any idea about how to farm," replied Shinichi.

Unfortunately, he'd been raised by white-collar workers in an average household, so he had no clue how to plant and harvest rice, catch large hauls of fish from the ocean, or slaughter cattle.

"Wouldn't it be more efficient to have the humans do all the labor and steal their bounty instead of starting from scratch? And also—," he said, summoning a devilish smile, "it'd be too kind and boring to kill those foolish, insubordinate humans and spare them from pain, right?"

He knew the sweet taste of victory would pair well with the feeling of terrifying the humans, forcing them into despair, and conquering them. It'd only be appropriate for the supreme ruler of the demon world—the Blue Demon King—to enjoy it, too.

"Ha-ha-ha, you're right. Shinichi, you're truly nefarious," declared the King with a cackle.

"Not as evil as Your Highness," flattered Shinichi, playing up the part of a criminal and pandering to the Demon King, who spoke like a corrupt cop.

Once Shinichi saw he'd expertly convinced the King, he looked over at Rino and—

"Shinichi, you're scarier than any demon alive...," she remarked.

"What—?!" He pretended to be evil for Rino and to save the humans from complete annihilation, but she'd taken his words to heart.

"Oh come on, my performance was perfect...!"

"*Too* perfect to be a performance."

Celes's response cut into him as he slumped back to his seat, shocked. But when he passed by Rino, she whispered quietly so only he could hear.

"Thank you, Shinichi." Her smile showed her gratitude—for his kindness and for pretending to be evil for her sake.

"Rino..." Shinichi's heart beat faster when he saw Rino's seriously angelic smile, but the maid's icy look and her father's murderous glare made him clear his throat and pretend nothing had happened. "Ahem... One other thing: You should forget about returning to the demon world for now," Shinichi said.

"Why would that be?" asked Rino.

"The humans might think you're running home in fear. If they do, they might get carried away and follow you back to attack the demon world," replied Shinichi.

He looked at Celes, who understood what he meant and expanded on it.

"If they're capable of teleportation, anyone can move between this world and the demon world. They don't know the location of the demon world yet, which is the only thing stopping them. But they could easily follow us into our world if they found any magical residue left behind. And seeing we've already teleported from this castle to the real one, it won't take them long."

If the humans came to the demon world, all hell would break loose...for the humans.

"Then all the bloodthirsty demons would go crazy and spill out into the human world. Would you be able to stop them, Your Highness?" asked Shinichi.

"What? I would have no desire to," he responded.

"Mm-hmm, just as I thought." The King didn't say he couldn't stop them.

"Ooh, if that happens, then the humans...," began Rino.

"They'd all be killed. In fact, they'd face complete annihilation with no chance to retreat," Shinichi finished for her.

If the humans chose to go to the demon world, they'd find hell. If they tried to retreat, they'd find hell. The humans weren't aware they'd be cornered either way.

"All I wanted was to eat tasty snacks. Why did it have to come to this...?" asked Rino as tears streamed down her face. Her selfish desires had caused the humans so much trouble.

"You're not in the wrong! You're good! The humans are the ones who are all bad!" bellowed the Demon King, attempting to console his daughter. He seemed unaware he was the cause of her tears.

Shinichi watched them from the corner of his eyes as he continued to talk to Celes.

"Let's get back on topic. How are we going to defeat those cheating, indestructible bastards? I'm just going to refer to them as the heroes for now," he clarified.

"That's the reason we called you. Now get to it, you idle good-for-nothing," she sneered.

"Stop making me sound like a NEET or something!" Shinichi was so fed up with Celes, who took every opportunity to insult him.

Whatever. He'd already found a solution to the problem.

"I've already thought of a way to defeat the heroes, but in order to do it, we need to round them up," he declared.

"Like capture them?" Celes asked, looking at her master.

Capturing them using the King's power should be simple enough. The main problem was keeping him from going overboard and killing them.

"I was thinking we should set some sort of trap for them. But before that, quick question: Where do these heroes come from?" questioned Shinichi.

"Hmm, I assume from where the humans live," said the King,

returning to the conversation after consoling his daughter. He held up his palm, projecting a satellite photograph of a bird's-eye view of the region out of thin air. "The center's my castle. This in the bottom right is the nearest human settlement. I imagine they come from here."

"You say nearest, but how many miles away is it?" asked Shinichi.

"About eighteen *goats* (thirty-five miles)," replied the King.

"It seems that our great teacher, Mr. Translate, even handles unit conversion," said Shinichi to himself, impressed again by the capabilities of this spell.

"They're probably respawning from there, but walking on an unpaved wild path for thirty-five miles? That'd be hard to do in a day, even if you trained hard enough. I guess that leaves us with magic," he concluded.

Teleportation spells were a convenient staple in the fantasy genre. In fact, he'd already seen the King use it a number of times in the short span he'd been here.

"Maybe they're teleporting?" offered Shinichi.

"Yeah, probably. What's so strange about that?" demanded the King.

"Nothing. Wait, is it really *that* easy to teleport?"

In many video games, the player needed to have some mastery of magic to teleport. Of course, there were some games that allowed you to teleport from the beginning to eliminate lengthy expositions and travel time. But teleportation was something that twenty-first-century science hadn't been able to manage. He naturally assumed it'd be difficult to do, even with the use of magic.

Once again, Celes answered Shinichi's question.

"No, it's not particularly easy. The King's just a special case," she explained.

"Ah, of course."

"Ha! My power is to be feared," butted in the King, trying in vain to show off.

Shinichi noticed the way the maid looked at the King, but kept his mouth shut. It was as if she'd seen some strange animal.

"Based on what you're saying, anyone can teleport with some difficulty, right?"

"Yes. If you spend a few hours drawing a magic circle at either terminal and commit them both to memory, it's possible to move between two points with ease," said Celes.

It still required natural-born talent and a few minutes of mental focus before a person could cast the spell. But the King could teleport anywhere without a magic circle or incantation. Shinichi was starting to learn just how powerful he was.

"I see, so they teleport to a magic circle...," murmured Shinichi.

"Do you intend to find the circle and destroy it?" inquired Celes.

"No, I won't destroy it." Shinichi immediately shot down her assumption.

Even if they destroyed the circle, the heroes could make another one somewhere more inconspicuous. They'd all just end up in a vicious cat and mouse game.

"No, we won't be destroying it," he repeated.

Shinichi had a better plan, and the corners of his mouth sprung up into a smile. His grin was more evil and sinister than the one on the Blue Demon King himself.

"All right! Let's get a move on!"

It was noon, and the red sun had reached its peak. The heroes began their daily routine by preparing for teleportation. They were in a mansion belonging to the knight, one of the Boar Kingdom's lower-class aristocrats.

"Okay, everyone, step into the magic circle."

The party followed the sorceress's orders and stepped into the massive magic circle, covering the floor of the entire room.

"I think the Demon King's gotten a lot weaker."

"Yeah, I'd like to finish him off in, like, five days," said the knight.

"...Really?" asked the warrior.

The knight nodded deeply in response to the warrior's short question.

"We'll be the ones to take down the Demon King. We're going to be granted land of our own and become earls. And I'm not going to let that be taken away from me by anyone," declared the knight.

"Yes, and we've gotten stronger over the past few days, thanks to these battles. Let's give it our all!" encouraged the priestess, agreeing wholeheartedly with the leader of their party. The two made a promise that they'd get married when this fight was over and the knight became an earl. It's only natural they were hopeful.

"That's enough chitchat for now. We're leaving," announced the sorceress. Her eyes had been closed all along, as she continued to concentrate on the *Teleport* spell.

"All right, we'll leave it to you," said the knight.

"You got it… We turn our bodies into light; take us to their land! *Teleport!*"

Her magical power accumulated, bursting into light and enveloping the party. Their vision twisted and tunneled, disorienting them and their sense of direction—left and right, up and down. A moment later, their surroundings changed into a magic circle inscribed near the Demon King's castle, where they…didn't appear.

"…Huh?"

The knight knew something was wrong, but it took a few seconds for his brain to take in this strange situation.

His eyes were open, but he couldn't see anything. He was in true darkness, blacker than the night.

"What the—? Was there some kind of mistake in the spell—?!"

He tried looking in the direction of the sorceress and then realized another problem.

He couldn't move his neck. No. He couldn't move his hands or his feet or his entire body. He couldn't move a single finger for that matter.

"What the—? What the hell is this?!"

He screamed in fear, but it rebounded from something directly in front of his eyes, ricocheting back and leaving his eardrums ringing.

That's when he noticed something else. His entire body was wrapped tightly in a hard substance. He couldn't move an inch.

"What *is* this…? Shit, move!"

He put all his might into moving his hands and legs, but it was completely pointless. Worse, his failed attempts quickened the onset of despair.

"Huff, huff… Can't breathe…"

There wasn't enough room for him to lift a single finger, and air was running out quickly in the confined space.

"Let me out…please… Get me out of here!"

He gathered the last of his strength to scream, but it was swallowed by the void and reached only his ears.

The only thing he could do was count the quiet footsteps of the Grim Reaper, approaching him from behind, and die without knowing what happened to him.

"All right! It looks like it went pretty well," said Shinichi, observing the heroes succumbing to despair just a few yards away. To be exact, he wasn't directly looking at the heroes themselves but rather the massive stone in which they were trapped.

"To think we could place a giant stone at their destination to close them in," marveled the King.

"What a dirty trick," sneered Celes.

The King, who'd moved the massive stone using magic, was quite impressed, and Celes, who found their location with a spell, wore an inscrutable expression as always.

"I call it the amazing 'Stuck in a Stone' strategy! It's their fault for using the *Teleport* spell without understanding its risks," explained Shinichi.

Having them teleport into a rock was a brutal trap, guaranteed to destroy even the most powerful party. Anyone familiar with a certain dungeon role-playing game would think to use this strategy—with some traumatic flashbacks. It was incredibly effective and gave the heroes no way to resist their impending doom.

"Yeah, it's lucky I played all those good old classics."

"I don't understand what you're saying. Anyway, what do we do with them now? Should I throw them into the mouth of a volcano?" asked the King.

"No. Like I said, we can't kill them. Can you remove them from the stone once they've lost consciousness?"

"Leave it to me."

Using magic, the King became clairvoyant to look into the stone. When all the heroes were unconscious, he struck the rock with a powerful punch.

"Humph!"

And just like that, cracks appeared in the boulder, taller than the King, and it shattered into millions of tiny pieces.

"I bet you'd be able to free yourself even if you were buried deep in the South Pole...," Shinichi speculated.

"South Pole... What's that?" asked the King.

"I'll explain later," he replied. "All right. Let's go back to the castle. The real fun starts now."

Shinichi and the others divvied up the unconscious heroes, carried them on their backs, and teleported back to the castle.

Later, the heroes would think back to this moment. If only they'd been lucky enough to suffocate to death.

"...Ugh, where am I?" groaned the knight as he slowly opened his eyes, glancing around at his surroundings in a daze.

In his field of view, he saw an unfamiliar stone room. Ironically, he was slightly relieved by this. Far better this than that black void. No sooner had he taken a moment to relax, however, than an unfamiliar voice whispered into his ear. It was as if someone had been waiting to catch him off guard.

"Have you finally woken up?"

"Who are you?!" demanded the knight. He reflexively tried to jump back, but his hands and feet pulled him off balance. His movements were accompanied by the irritating sound of clanking metal, and he finally realized he'd been shackled to a wall.

"Ack!"

"It seems you finally understand your predicament. Don't worry, your friends are unharmed."

The knight looked to his side and saw the other four chained to the wall. Their eyes opened slowly at the commotion.

"Hey, what the hell is this?!"

"Have we been captured?"

"...Hmph."

The ranger, priestess, and warrior all cried out in bewilderment as they tried to grasp the situation. But as the figure had said, everyone was fine.

Well, with the exception of one person.

"Let me out... It's dark, no, it hurts, I'm scared, let me out, let me out...," the sorceress kept muttering, unaware of her companions around her. Her eyes were glazed over. She'd lost her marbles upon being trapped in stone.

"Mirida!" shouted the knight.

"So her name is Mirida? She must be claustrophobic. I'm truly sorry about that. I had no intention of pushing her to the breaking point."

"You arrogant asshole! Show yourself!" barked the knight at the mysterious voice, presumably the mastermind behind this entire operation. He couldn't tell where it was coming from.

As it turned out, the voice emanated from a rather unexpected direction.

"I wasn't trying to hide or anything. I'm above you," it said.

"What?!"

Looking up, the knight saw there was no ceiling. Instead, a solitary figure, concealed entirely in a black cloak, stood on the edge of the wall. The only thing clearly visible about the monster was its white mask and the sinister smile drawn upon it.

"I am the Blue Demon King's Dirty Advisor. My name is—well, you can call me Smile."

"Smile, what an eerie name..." The knight gulped, nervous.

Shinichi—or Smile—was undaunted as he grinned behind his mask and looked down at the petrified knight.

It's interesting they're scared of the untranslated word smile. *I wonder what they'd think of Shinichi Sotoyama? Rino said it sounded odd, but what would the humans think?*

He was admittedly a bit curious, but chose to focus on the task at hand.

"First of all, I would like to apologize that we must converse under such terrible conditions. This was the only way, however, you seemed willing to talk to us."

"Talk?" inquired the knight.

"That's right. I believe there's been a misunderstanding between us," replied Shinichi.

The knight sternly glared at him as if to say he had no business talking to demons, but Shinichi continued speaking, completely disregarding the knight's menacing stare.

"What do you think about us demons?" he asked.

"What do I think…? That you're savages and dangerous monsters who crawl out from the depths of the earth!" cried the ranger.

"You're the kin of the Evil God, sealed deep underground with the Evil Dragon. Tens of thousands of years ago, he was banished there, defeated by the Divine Goddess," accused the priestess.

Shinichi smiled to himself as he gleaned new information from the ranger and priestess.

So the demons come from deep within the earth…which means the demon world is underground. And there've been times when demons came up to their world in the past.

To be clear, this situation started when Rino's mother appeared in the human world. She was apparently picking fights with those who crossed her path. To her, she was benevolently flexing her skills, but to the people she attacked, she was a truly terrifying presence. If similar events had happened before, it's no wonder the humans saw the demons as their enemies.

"I see. It seems my brethren have caused much trouble for you. I do apologize for that. However, I would like you to understand that we, the members of the Blue Demon King's clan, have no desire to fight you."

He apologized before expressing his hope of reconciliation. If they accepted his peace offering, their futile fighting would be put to rest. But just as Shinichi had expected, the knight rejected it completely.

"Cut the crap! Don't try to feed us this bullshit after everything that's happened!"

"That's because you attacked us without warning," said Shinichi.

"Of course we're going to attack! You slaughtered three thousand of our soldiers!"

"Ah, well, were you not the ones who sent your army to slaughter our brethren?"

"Tch… If we hadn't, you bastards would have attacked us. You're the ones who invaded our territory, and you're in the wrong for occupying Dog Valley!"

"It's located in a distant area, a full two-day walk from your kingdom. Not a single person lives here, and there are no roads nor signs. You call this narrow, untamed valley your territory? Do you have any proof?"

"Proof or no proof, these mountains were conquered by our kingdom's founder, Tortoise I! It's Boar Kingdom's territory!"

"Hmm… I'll admit it was our fault for building our castle without properly investigating how the national boundaries are defined. Whatever. I arranged for us to meet to discuss this: Would it be possible for us to lower our swords and peacefully discuss a monetary solution?"

"This entire world belongs to the Divine Goddess and humankind! There isn't a shred of land we'd give you vile demons!"

No matter what Shinichi said, the knight shot down all of his proposals.

This isn't working. We'll never be on the same page.

Even though Shinichi was giving up this method, he was still satisfied with the new information he'd gleaned. Based on the knight's attitude and answers, it was clear the demons had told him the truth: The humans had attacked first.

I'm not saying the demons are blameless, but it's clear the humans are definitely in the wrong. Great. This means I don't have to go easy on them.

Even though they were in a totally different world, he was aware they were all connected as human beings. He was raised with morals and social standards in Japan, a peaceful, law-governed country. But he had more than enough reason to throw that all aside. He was the Demon King's Dirty Advisor, after all, and he smiled menacingly beneath his mask.

"That's a shame. I'd hoped we could abandon our prejudices and build a positive relationship…," he said.

That would've been the best outcome—appeasing Rino, too—but there wasn't much he could do if the heroes themselves rejected his offer.

"If you're saying you're going to continue attacking us, you leave me with no choice but to destroy you," Shinichi warned.

"Ha! See if you can!" the ranger retorted with a snort.

He wouldn't be able to kill them—well, even if he did, they'd just come back to life. They were immortal, therefore invincible. There was no way they'd lose, which guaranteed they'd eventually defeat the almighty Demon King.

Shinichi let out a snicker at the sight of the cocky heroes.

"Don't misunderstand me. I never once said I would 'kill you.' I said I'd 'end you' and your capacity to respawn over and over again, you fiendish insects," he said.

"……"

The knight picked up on his strange word choice. Silently, he began gathering his magical powers, preparing to cast a certain spell, but Shinichi saw right through his hardened expression.

"Oh, I won't let you do that," said Shinichi, gently raising his hand and signaling to Celes, who'd been waiting silently behind him the whole time.

With his cue, the talented maid understood, jumped down in front of the knight, and lifted him up by his neck.

"Gah—!"

"Were you planning to kill yourself to escape this place? You really don't want to do that. This area's under a special magic field. If you die here, you can't be resurrected," taunted Shinichi.

"What?!"

"Y-you're bluffing!" shouted the ranger.

"Feel free to test it out," Shinichi calmly replied.

"……Tsk."

Even though he'd spoken forcefully a moment before, the ranger fell silent in the face of Shinichi's confidence. The whole magic field thing was a lie, of course. Shinichi even anticipated the heroes would see through it, but that was all part of the plan. If there was even a small doubt that maybe, just maybe, it was true, they wouldn't be able to kill themselves as easily, which bought Shinichi more time.

All right. Here we go.

To defeat an immortal monster, the "Make It Impossible to Move and Seal It Away for All of Eternity" strategy was the most popular method. For example, one could encase its body in iron and sink it into the depths of the ocean. Though not dead, the creature would be rendered harmless.

This method worked well for immortals but less so for those who could be brought back to life. It's hard to say it'd be impossible, but they'd need constant monitoring to keep them from killing themselves. So it really wasn't a practical solution.

"I can break you down mentally so you lack the will to fight back anymore," mumbled Shinichi.

"…Ah!" The priestess's body shook in terror at Shinichi's quiet words.

"Do you intend to torture us? Ha! Give us your best shot!" The knight broke free from Celes's hand and let out a shout, as if to console the priestess.

"Hmm. Brave, aren't you?" observed Shinichi.

"Lord Smile," said Celes, leaping nimbly to Shinichi's side and whispering a warning in his ear. "Torture's pointless. All of them are under the *Pain Block* spell at all times."

"I'm not surprised." This answered another question that'd been lingering in the depths of his heart.

Even if one could come back to life, no one would want to experience and writhe in pain from deadly injuries. This was the reason these heroes removed their sense of pain, as they faced the King day in and day out.

This would also explain why they're able to continue fighting even if they're in a critical condition of, like, 1 HP.

Shinichi switched to his backup plan.

"The word *torture* isn't just limited to physical pain," said Shinichi, turning to face the priestess with his creepy mask.

"Ah!" She shrieked in horror.

"Defiling a young maiden and using her body for your own pleasure? Definitely the sickest and dirtiest method," said Celes.

"I didn't say that! Well, actually, it crossed my mind, but I wasn't actually going to do it!" Shinichi shot back, out of character for a moment, responding to the maid's scornful look. He coughed before continuing. "...What I'm talking about is even more terrifying than torture. Let's see. How about putting a large number of *these* in that hole you're in?" he proposed, reaching into his cloak to produce a glass bottle, containing something he'd found in the castle.

The thing in the vial made a rasping sound as it ran around, the light glistening off its slimy—

"Gyaaaah—!"

A deep, earsplitting scream suddenly echoed throughout the room. Surprised, Shinichi looked to see where it'd come from and saw the silent warrior and his brawny body quivering in fear.

"P-p-please, not that... I'll do anything..."

"So if I asked you not to attack again—," began Shinichi.

"I promise! So just get that black thing..."

"Huh, seriously?" asked Shinichi, confused by the tears welling up in the warrior's eyes and his willingness to give in to Shinichi's demands. "But what if I just put it in there with you? Put some cuts on your body, slathered on some honey, let her eat from your wounds, lay eggs—"

"S-st-stooop—!" The warrior let out a high-pitched, girlie scream, then passed out upon listening to Shinichi casually explain his torture method of choice.

"Dammit! It's really low of you to intimidate Goldeo with a bug!"

"I can't believe we're parting ways like this…"

"I mean, if the bug came up to me, I'd also…"

"You're all fine with this?" inquired Shinichi, exasperated the heroes would so easily accept their comrade's fate.

"I can't believe he's that afraid of a little roach. Right?" Shinichi looked to Celes in solidarity.

"Please don't come any closer," said Celes, her face pale. In the next moment, she suddenly moved to the opposite end of the room.

What a sad creature, always despised, even in this world…

When he'd found the cockroach in the castle halls, Shinichi'd actually felt a bit homesick to encounter a familiar creature. That said, he wasn't particularly fond of cockroaches, either, which was why he'd caught the pest in a bottle, fully intending to dispose of it later.

"Well, whatever. Now that this pair is pretty much useless, have you two decided not to attack us anymore?" asked Shinichi, turning to the knight and priestess. "If not, I'll be forced to do something horrible, something that can't be undone."

"I refuse to succumb to you and your ulterior motives! It's our divine duty as the heroes of the Divine Goddess to root out and eliminate demonkind!" cried the knight.

"Heroes, huh…" He was a bit taken aback they'd refer to themselves as *heroes*. Shinichi had only used the term for convenience sake, based off video games.

Anyway, he'd already made his decision.

"It seems we have no choice. Please use *that*," he commanded.

"Understood, Lord Smile," replied Celes, who bowed and jumped in front of the knight once more. With her left hand, she pried the knight's cheeks apart, and with her right hand, she pulled a vial from her pocket, forcing him to drink its contents.

"Ugh, gah…ack, pah… Poison is pointless," he sputtered.

Poison would only help him die and resurrect elsewhere. But Shinichi gazed at the brave knight with amusement.

"I guess you could say it's a kind of poison. But we'll see if it's as pointless as you say."

"What do you mea— Ack!" yelped the knight, his face suddenly white as a sheet.

"Leader, what's wrong?!" asked the priestess.

"Put a spell on me to—," he began to reply.

"I won't let you," interrupted Shinichi.

Celes stopped the priestess from interfering. Her spells would've been pointless anyway. They all watched as the knight broke out in a greasy sweat, body trembling.

"Agh…gah, ngah!"

"I'll explain in place of our poor knight here. He's just consumed a concoction made from *chekin* berries," said Shinichi.

"*Chekin* berries?" asked the ranger.

These berries didn't exist in the human world, so the heroes hadn't heard of them before.

"It's the fruit of a plant from the demon world. It's incredibly disgusting, of course, but it's better known for having a particular side effect, handy when you're sitting between two ladies," continued Shinichi.

"Ladies…? It can't be!" cried the priestess.

Shinichi grinned demonically at her as she finally understood.

"Yeah, it's a medicine that makes you really have to go. In other words, it's a laxative."

Guborgyuu—u!

The knight's stomach made a strange sound as if in agreement, reverberating throughout the chamber, as the berries completely destroyed him from within.

"P-please let me out of these chains!"

"You're the one who brushed aside the hand of friendship. You're pushing your luck," replied Shinichi sadly.

"Ack, gah… But as a knight, as the Goddess's hero, to give in to evil demons would…ah!"

"Your resolve is commendable. Then I guess soiling yourself isn't too bad, right?"

"Bu…but—but…ah!"

The knight gritted his teeth and tried to endure the pain, looking at the priestess—the woman he loved, the one who'd promised to become his wife once all this was over. Her face was very pale with fear, but her eyes wouldn't leave his.

In front of the love of his life, the knight finally—

"Don't look! Oh, please don't look...agh, aaaah—!"

"Guh, ugh..."

A few minutes later, the hole was filled with a strange and disgusting smell, the sound of a man sobbing, and the five heroes.

"How pathetic. An adult openly crying in front of other people," scolded Shinichi.

"You say that as if you're not the one who did this to him. You're sick," said Celes, exasperated.

Called out by Celes once again, Shinichi lowered his brows.

"You think so? I've heard stories about rookie soldiers wetting themselves from fear and first-class snipers waiting for their target for three or four days. They don't move a muscle, even if they soil themselves. You know what's really sick? The fact that they'd be more eager to kill people than dirty themselves with their own poop," he replied.

Shinichi just could not understand how someone could casually kill another intelligent creature, even if it was a different species.

"All right. Let's show them something nice now," he suggested, holding out an item to the heroes. It'd coincidentally been in his uniform pocket when he'd been summoned into this world and was the closest man-made thing to magic.

"This is a magic tool called a smartphone. It can capture the images and sounds and re-create them indefinitely."

"Smartphone?" echoed the priestess, peering into the mysterious object.

Shinichi expressionlessly pressed the button to replay the video.

"Don't look! Oh, please don't look…agh, aaaah—!'"

"S-stop—!" cried the knight, waking up to the sounds of his intestinal destruction. They echoed throughout the room once again, and the Dirty Advisor of the Blue Demon King made no move to stop them.

"I wonder what'd happen if we projected this video in the sky, right above your country," Shinichi speculated deviously.

"What?!"

"The Brown Knight or the Manure Pit Hero… I'm sure they'll mock you with nicknames."

"Ack!"

"Even if you manage to defeat the Demon King, even if you become the hero who saved the world, even if your name goes down in history, people will always laugh at you. You know, where I'm from, there was a general who united the land but made one little mistake. It's been more than four hundred years since his death, but people are still laughing at him," cackled Shinichi, thinking about how scary history was, while holding up the smartphone. "So if you attack us again—"

"I won't! I swear! So please…," interrupted the knight, begging between heavy sobs.

"Leader…," intoned the ranger, disappointed by the pathetic sight.

But the priestess turned to the defiled knight with a look of tenderness.

"Ruzal, lift your face. Everyone's bound to soil themselves in front of others. Think about babies or those approaching death in old age. You need not worry," she said.

"But an adult doing this…"

"You did nothing wrong. It's simply a result of a lowly plan carried out by the demons. You've nothing to be ashamed of. You fight for the people, and you're a magnificent hero of the Goddess…and the man I love."

"Minya…," said the knight, forgetting his soiled lower half. He basked under her saintly smile and gazed into his lover's eyes.

Seeing the moving scene unfold in front of him, Shinichi bowed his head and—

"Actually, I think I'll make this public," he announced.

"Aaa—ah?!"

"You're the worst." Celes's voice dripped with disgust as the masked advisor made no attempt to conceal his jealousy of the couple in love.

Chapter 3

The Main Act Is to Come

The audience chambers were on the top floor of the king's castle, built in the very center of Boar Kingdom. In the middle of this room, King Tortoise IV rose from his throne in shock.

"Are the heroes actually missing?!"

"Yes, Ruzal and the other four heroes have left Boar Kingdom," reported the commander, deeply distressed and uncertain whether or not he himself believed it. "They sent word that the responsibility of defeating the Demon King was far too great, and the five of them left the kingdom, going their separate ways."

"Ridiculous! Ruzal is the heir of a great and noble house. Are you saying he'd throw away his inheritance and title?!"

"Yes. He said, 'I've found something more precious than land and honor.'"

"That's absurd..." Displeased, Tortoise IV sank back onto his throne. "All five heroes leaving at the same time..."

Under the Goddess's guardianship, the heroes were an important military force, not only against monsters and demons but against neighboring countries as well. Only those with outstanding talent could become heroes. They had immense magical prowess, and they could take on a thousand enemies at once, single-handedly influencing the fate of the country. And now the kingdom was losing five of them at once, which made even the king's face pale.

"Were you unable to stop them? No, it's not too late. Go and bring them back using any means necessary," ordered Tortoise IV. He wouldn't punish them for their failure to defeat the Demon King. In fact, he'd go so far as to offer them a monetary gift as an apology for forcing them to take on an impossible task. He'd even offer Ruzal the title of earl he so desired.

The commander shook his head with a pained look as his king desperately threw out suggestions.

"I fear it will not work. I've attempted to stop them and persuade them to change their minds, but they're steadfast in their decision..."

The knight had already abandoned the most important thing to him: his family. Nothing could sway a decision that immense.

"Above all else, they're absolutely petrified of the Demon King. According to them, 'He's a creature more wicked than the Evil God himself, and we're no match for him...,'" continued the commander.

To be exact, the heroes were actually afraid of the Demon King's advisor, but there was no way the commander could know that.

"Are you saying the Demon King's so horrifying the heroes would throw away everything?!" asked the king incredulously.

"I was under the impression Your Highness was also well aware of this."

"Mm..." The king let out a long groan and fell silent.

They were talking about the same Demon King who'd single-handedly defeated three thousand soldiers. Both the king and his commander, who'd led the remaining shreds of that army, had seen an immense power beyond their worst nightmares.

"An embodiment of true horror, as you would expect from his title...," murmured the king.

The army had pushed forth in high spirits after breezily dispatching the orcs and goblins. Those ugly monsters were as weak as legend would have them. But then the army came face-to-face with that blue giant, who raised one hand and spoke some incantation. In the next moment, arrows of light rained from the sky, moving of their own accord and piercing the hearts of three thousand soldiers. In the length of a short breath, they were killed and utterly defeated.

"How much power does he have...?"

His controlled attack left the bodies of the slain soldiers intact, striking even more fear into the hearts of those who remained. Had the bodies been injured any further, resurrection would've been impossible, unless they were heroes, of course. The Demon King must've known this, as all the soldiers sustained only a single injury.

It's kind of like how it's harder to take an enemy alive than to kill them. It's even harder to kill your enemy and leave an undamaged corpse. And yet, with incredible ease, that's what the Demon King did. In other words, if he'd intended to kill them, he could've destroyed not just half the army but the entire army and kingdom, eradicating everyone, including Tortoise IV. They'd encountered a demon of great strength, just as legend had it—no, *more* powerful than in those stories.

Were they fighting an impossible battle?

Should they surrender themselves as quickly as possible?

"We shouldn't have faced the demons..." The king quietly uttered these cowardly words.

"What're you saying, Your Highness?" chimed in a man in his early thirties who'd been standing at the king's side with a serene smile on his face. He wore a pure-white robe emblazoned with a golden symbol reminiscent of the sun. He carried no sword and wore no armor. "Our Goddess will not look kindly on us if we overlook the demons and their sins."

"O-of course, Bishop Hube." Tortoise IV becamc flustered when he saw the bishop's smile. At first glance, it appeared benevolent, but it carried a quiet forcefulness, allowing no room for excuses or objections. "We, the faithful followers of the Divine Goddess, would never yield to those foul demons!"

"Hmm, I see. All is well."

Tortoise IV rubbed his chest in relief upon receiving a pardon from Bishop Hube, as the commander and other ministers displayed visible displeasure at the pathetic sight of their king. They didn't dare say anything, though. The pope and other high-ranking cardinals were the only people in this country—actually, in this world—who could take a stand against a Goddess's bishop.

"However, it's unforgivable for the heroes, for the Goddess's disciples, to flee from evil," said Bishop Hube in a hellishly calm voice. "Let us contact the church to have Ruzal and the others excommunicated."

"What…?!" Tortoise IV let out a cry of shock, and the others froze in response to this callous decision.

There's always at least one church for the Goddess in every territory. This was true, of course, for great cities like Boar Kingdom but also for small towns with a couple hundred residents. The church wasn't just a pillar of faith: It was an institution that literally held life itself in its very hands. It healed disease and injury and gave back life to those who died. To be excommunicated meant they could never enter the church again. In other words, it meant they'd never again be resurrected.

In normal cases, one could be resurrected as long as the body was intact. But this security blanket would be taken away if one was excommunicated. Faced with this fear, not even the king could go against the Goddess's bishops.

"But Ruzal and the others are heroes. Excommunication would…"

As heroes chosen by the Goddess and granted the power of immortality, wouldn't it be pointless to kick them out?

Bishop Hube beamed as he spoke to Tortoise IV.

"As believers of the Goddess, we know best how to handle heroes," said Hube. He didn't provide any more details, and his excessively wide smile was anything but comforting.

"Th-that's good, then…," stammered the king.

"Yes, Your Highness has nothing to be concerned about," reassured Hube, turning from the king, who could do nothing but agree with him. He looked toward the entrance. "A true hero will grant our prayers and defeat the evil demons," he insisted.

Just as he finished saying this, the large door to the audience chamber opened, and a lone figure walked in—a swordswoman with flaming red hair and a matching crimson scarf.

What she lacked in grace, she had in energy. In light clothing, she came to a full stop in front of the king, respectfully took a knee, and spoke with a strong, clear voice.

"Arian, hero of the Divine Goddess, reporting back from my duties as ordered by the church! The great black wolf has been exterminated!"

"I'm glad to see you've returned safely," said Hube, momentarily taking his attention off the king.

Arian was unsure if she'd interrupted their conversation, but she simply flashed a smile before dropping and opening her sack. From her bag, she withdrew a fang, the length of a grown man's forearm. With one look, the audience saw the size and brutality of the black wolf she'd single-handedly fought. The fang served as proof of her skills.

"Ah, that's amazing! As I'd expect from Miss Arian!" crooned the commander.

"Thank you very much," she replied with an embarrassed smile.

As Hube watched this exchange, his smile hardened slightly. He quickly changed the topic, asking her, "So, Arian, you've been away from the kingdom, but I am sure you've heard the rumors."

"Are you talking about the stories about demons in Dog Valley?" she asked.

"Precisely. An army of evil demons is attempting to steal our land and slaughter our people."

He failed to say that Boar Kingdom had mobilized their army first and continued the attack with their five heroes. He also made a point to not mention he'd pushed for the use of force, despite the king's repeated insistence they proceed with caution.

"So the demons continue to do such horrible things...," said Arian, taking Hube's words as truth. She hung her head as a dark expression overtook her face.

"Yes, and as the Goddess has taught us, the demons are hideous, barbaric filth that must be eliminated," continued Hube.

"......"

"The five heroes, including Ruzal, attempted to eliminate our enemy, but they feared the Demon King to such a degree that they ran and abandoned their country."

"What? Sir Ruzal and the others?!" exclaimed Arian.

"Unfortunately, it's the truth," said Hube. He didn't mention they'd be excommunicated from the church and continued with a gentle voice. "Arian, you're the only one who can save our country. Will you defeat the demons?"

"……"

Arian was silent for a moment and wore a complicated expression, but she raised her head and looked at Tortoise IV. After all, the king carried the burden of governing and guiding this country. Under her serene, saintly gaze, though, Tortoise IV couldn't help but feel inferior to her.

He didn't have a choice. He had to deliver his order.

"Hero Arian, I hereby order you to defeat the Demon King in Dog Valley."

"At your command, even if it takes my life!"

Even though she'd just come back from killing the black wolf, Arian showed no indication of fatigue, accepting the king's orders with a dazzlingly bright smile. She stood, bowed once, and quickly left the audience chamber to start her new journey.

Grinning, Hube watched her slim figure depart.

"Those despicable demons are as good as dead. Our Goddess has watched over and protected the peace of Boar Kingdom once again," he said.

After Arian defeated the Demon King, her accomplishments would be attributed to him, making him an archbishop—though he obviously didn't say as much. Watching him, Tortoise IV saw through his ulterior motives and sighed as he stared after the hero as she disappeared.

Oh, Arian... You're too pure and good a child for the blackhearted bishop.

He was disgusted at their current circumstances and himself for pushing her to fight the ruthless blue giant. There was only a one-in-a-million chance of defeating him.

But if there was anyone who could do so, it was her. That's precisely why he couldn't stop her.

"But she's only a young maiden..."

Her red hair cascaded down her shoulders as the swordswoman, one of the most powerful magic users in all of Boar Kingdom, walked with pride.

The fact that she was so young pained the king's heart even more.

"Ba-ha-ha! Well done, my advisor!" exclaimed the Demon King.

At long last, the attacks from the heroes had ended, and peace returned to the castle. To celebrate the occasion, the King held a grand banquet.

"It's all thanks to you, Shinichi. I really can't thank you enough," beamed Rino.

"I'd also like to thank you from the bottom of my heart," said Celes, bowing her head deeply to show her gratitude while maintaining her stony expression.

"Yeah—! You saved us all, *moo*!"

"Now I can finally get to work on farming, *oink*."

"Thank you so much!"

"Hmm, shall I do something *nice* to show my appreciation?"

At the banquet, Kalbi and Sirloin also offered their praise, alongside many other demons in the human world, including a snake woman and a girl with devil-like wings and a tail. (At least, he *thought* it was a girl.) All of them thanked Shinichi for managing to chase away the heroes, though he was more uncomfortable receiving so much praise than being surrounded by such a large crowd.

"Thanks, but this solution's only temporary," he said.

To make sure the five heroes would never come back, Celes cast a *Gaes* spell on them before letting them go. To do so, the other party first had to consent to its conditions, but once cast, it couldn't be broken, so it was unlikely the heroes would bother them again. Of course, there were ways to break the spell, but finding someone powerful enough to undo Celes's magic would be tough. She was second only to the King. And on top of that, the heroes had nothing to gain from challenging the King again. However—

"That's enough talk. Drink up! Today, we celebrate!" bellowed the King, letting out a lively burst of laughter to get Shinichi to loosen up. He encouraged him to take a swig.

"There's a bunch of dishes, too," remarked Rino.

"I went into the forest to find ingredients from the human world. I hope you find these foods suit your palate," said Celes as she and Rino piled food on a plate to pass to him.

"Ah, thank you," he said, expressing his thanks as he took the plate, but his expression was still a bit strained.

The food at the "banquet" didn't live up to its name: It was a somewhat meager spread.

They only have water. And is this boar meat and boiled butterbur?

The meat hadn't been properly drained, carrying a strong, gamy smell in its congealed blood. They also neglected to remove the bitterness from the butterbur, rendering them inedible. But—

"Wow! Even the water from the human world tastes amazing!"

"I can't believe I get to eat such delicious meat! I'm so glad I came to this world, *moo*!"

"These vegetables are so good, too! I'll never be able to go back to the demon world, *oink*!"

Raving about the food, the Demon King and his inferiors continued laughing in joy and merriment.

Well, I guess it's a real treat if you compare it to their questionable dishes back home.

Out of some perverse curiosity, he'd wanted to sneak into their world to see their food, but he knew he probably wasn't going to have an opportunity to do so.

Especially since I'll be going back to Earth once this banquet's over. Lend us your power to defeat the heroes who can indefinitely resurrect. That's what he'd been asked to do, and now that he'd been successful, there was nothing keeping him here. *I know I'm an outsider, and I might cause some problems if I get too involved. But—*

Even though he could now return to Japan, he wasn't feeling very happy. He knew the reason why, but he tried to drown his emotions with a glass of water.

At that exact moment, he heard the sound of the door to the banquet hall opening.

"Your Highness, we have an emergency, *woof*!"

"This situation… It can't be…!" Shinichi had a bad feeling when he saw the disturbed expression on the dogheaded kobold.

"There's a strong human I've never seen before coming this way, *woof*!"

"Of course," said Shinichi, head in his hands upon hearing the report he feared would come. While they may have defeated the five heroes, there was no guarantee that there weren't others.

"…Maggots. Of course, they've come to disrespect me," muttered the King. He crushed his cup in a murderous rage, angry they'd arrived to ruin the mood. Wind swept around him as he shouted above it, "They certainly have some nerve! If they wish to die so much, I'll just kill them all!"

"Your Highness, please! Only the heroes—" Shinichi tried to ask the King to spare the humans from complete annihilation, but the King left via a *Teleport* spell halfway through his plea.

"Shinichi…," murmured Rino, peeking at his face uneasily.

"Ah well, he causes me trouble, too," said Shinichi, patting her head with a pained smile.

They stood there for five minutes before the King teleported back. Five minutes was definitely not enough time to wipe out all humanity, so Shinichi let out a sigh of relief.

Next to him, Rino let out a small shriek.

"Daddy, your arm!"

"Hmm? Oh, I'm bleeding," he said, noticing the blue blood trickling down his left arm.

"Wh-what the—?!" Shinichi cried out in shock at the sight of the unbelievable scene in front of him.

Yes, the cut was so small it could hardly be called an injury, and it disappeared without a trace when the King shook his arm. But this was the same Demon King who'd been completely uninjured by the combined attacks of the five heroes. Something or someone was strong enough to injure him. This was serious enough to make everyone in the room freeze in shock.

"The human who arrived today had a really strong backbone. We had a bit of fun before the hero ran away," laughed the King. His previously sour mood disappeared completely, replaced with a childlike excitement toward his shiny new toy.

"Hey, this isn't something to be happy about!" exclaimed Shinichi. The King was making light of a dangerous situation. Someone could actually hurt him. Shinichi couldn't contain his worries and fears, but the demons' reactions were entirely different.

"Huh, it's pretty impressive a human would be able to hurt Your Highness, *moo*!"

"What kind of fighting style did they use, *oink*? Please tell us, *oink*!"

"Ha-ha-ha, I'll tell you everything. Now don't be so hasty," the King playfully warned the excited pack of demons crowding around him.

"No. No, what's with this reaction?!" interrupted Shinichi, overwhelmed with disbelief.

The maid stared at him as if he were the strange one.

"Yes, this person is an enemy, strong enough to rival the King. But people of great strength are venerable and virtuous. What's your problem?" she asked.

"Whaaat!" erupted Shinichi in a daze upon hearing Celes was also a muscle-headed warmonger. His last hope lay with Rino, but when he looked over at her, he saw a complicated expression that suggested resignation.

"I don't think it's right they can do whatever they want just because they're strong...," Rino pointed out. But she knew that this was the status quo. Their world had a dog-eat-dog mentality, and she didn't say it with much force or conviction.

We have some things in common, like the desire to eat good food. But they're a completely different species with completely different customs, after all...

Even on Shinichi's home planet, one could experience culture shock by the simple act of crossing an ocean, and people were up in arms all the time for so-called peace or human rights. But it was always the strongest who resolved these conflicts and became the hero. Perhaps the demons had it easier. At least they didn't try to save face.

As Shinichi was lost in his train of thought, the King finished recounting the story, turning toward him.

"Well, that was an unexpected development," he said, "but let's continue with the celebration. You've done much for us, and it'd reflect poorly on me as the Blue Demon King if I didn't properly show my gratitude before you left."

"...Huh?" Shinichi found himself at a momentary loss for words. He hadn't anticipated this. "I'm allowed to leave?"

"Well, yes, I originally called you to handle that irritating lot."

"But there's a new hero now, right?"

"There is, but this one was clever enough to withdraw upon realizing the difference in our power. I don't imagine this human'll engage in the same idiotic plan as the last ones."

He must have picked up on something during their battle. He seemed certain the new challenger wasn't going to rely on rapid-succession resurrection.

"But..." Shinichi was uncertain if he should even say this aloud. "If this hero gets stronger and comes back, what happens if you lose—or die?"

The King was undeniably the most powerful being in this world. But even though he wasn't capable of aging or dying, he certainly wasn't invincible. After all, his newest challenger was strong enough to injure him. If that person got stronger and gathered allies of equal strength, he could be defeated once and for all. Could the King really just ignore someone trying to kill him?

Any normal human would think of some other way to eliminate the threat, but this was a different world, and Shinichi's sense of normalcy just didn't apply here. And to top it all off, he was talking to the King of the demon world.

"If I lose—and I honestly cannot imagine that happening—there's nothing I can do. The strongest wins and takes everything; the weakest is defeated and loses everything. That's the way of this world," mused the King without an inkling of fear on his face. Rather, he seemed eager to fight an opponent who could really challenge him.

"I see. As expected from the Demon King." Shinichi admired the straightforwardness of his resolve.

I wonder if the Demon Kings in video games feel the same way.

He was too weak willed to fully understand the Demon King's words, but he had no desire to belittle or criticize him. Looking around, he saw not only Celes but also the orcs and minotaurs agreeing with their King. Only Rino's face looked doubtful, but she expressed no uneasiness or disapproval.

No one was trying to keep Shinichi here. The tightness in his chest was his own fears and anxieties.

What'll happen to them if I go home?

Would they all end up dead at the hands of stronger heroes? Or would the King be able to keep fending them off? Would they give up and flee back to the demon world? Or would they call another human like Shinichi? There were so many possibilities.

And some of them would end in catastrophe.

Then again, he couldn't guarantee he could help them push back and win. If Shinichi were prioritizing his own life, he'd return to Japan, to safety and peace. That was the only certainty.

But can I be happy if I leave now?

The King, Rino, Celes, all the other demons he'd met and spoken with—they could all die. If he was the only one safe, could he act like it never happened and be happy again?

No, that'd be terrible.

For a moment, the image of a smiling young girl floated in his mind, and Shinichi slowly shook his head. He didn't care that much about others. He was simply a selfish human.

In fact, there were children on the other side of Earth who were starving to death or thrown onto battlefields with weapons. Yet, he could eat just fine, play his games, and sleep in his warm bed without feeling any sort of guilt, just like any normal human.

His feelings weren't about justice or integrity. Quite the contrary.

His motivation was a very egocentric reason: *I'd be sad to know my friends died.*

He knew very well how wrong it was to join forces with the demons to wreak havoc on his own kind. He knew an outsider shouldn't get so involved in another world. He knew what the established social standards were.

But he had no desire to yield to them. He was an average, twisted person, a far cry from some sort of saint. He just wanted to share joy with people he liked and laugh at the misery of those he didn't, and most of all—

It'd be really boring to leave now.

Shinichi's mouth stretched into a big smirk. He'd been summoned to a fantasy world to act as an advisor to the Demon King. There's no way he'd choose to end such a rare, wonderful experience in just a few days.

It's not like I have any dreams to fulfill back on Earth anyway.

He didn't have grand goals or skills to become someone like an athlete or a chemist. And it went without saying he didn't have a girlfriend. He was a little concerned his parents might be worried, but they really shouldn't expect any more from their idiot son. He didn't need to be told his life would be in danger. People died when their time came. He'd learned that ten years ago.

With all this in mind, he began verbalizing his inner desires into existence.

"Your Highness, may I request my reward for defeating the heroes?" he asked with grand formality.

"Hmm, oh yes. You may have anything you wish—other than my daughter," the King cautiously warned, sensing a sudden change in Shinichi's voice.

Without a word, the boy put on the mask with the twisted smile to say, "Well then, please command me to defeat the new hero."

"Shinichi, you...," began the King.

"What?!" yelped Rino. Looking at his masked face, the two uttered their surprise.

"Is this what you wish for?" asked Celes with a faint shadow of doubt on her normally impassive face. There was a chance this frail human boy would be destroyed beyond resurrection if he chose to accompany them. "Would it not be better for you to go home and drink your little sister's milk?"

"Stop making everything about sex! Also! I'm an only child!" Shinichi laughed with some force. This might have been her way of expressing concern. "I'm staying because my food won't taste as good tomorrow if I chose to abandon lovely ladies like you and Rino."

"Shinichi...," said Rino, blushing, almost moved to tears by his sudden compliment.

Even the corners of Celes's mouth twitched ever so slightly.

"In other words, you'd like to drink Lady Rino's milk?" she asked nefariously.

"What the—?!"

"What?! But I don't even have breasts yet!" objected Rino.

"Shinichi, come over here for a moment," snarled the King.

Looking back at Rino's bright red face, Shinichi tried to get the conversation back on track.

"Anyway! Your Highness, please allow your masked advisor Smile to defeat the hero. I'll drive away any who dare trouble you and Lady Rino," Shinichi declared, putting on an air of righteousness as he delivered this line.

Following his lead and finally understanding his resolve, the King spoke in a serious voice.

"Fine, then. The Blue Demon King, Ludabite Krolow Semah, orders you to use your wisdom and defeat the fool who stands against us demons!" he announced.

"Understood!"

"Also, get my lovely daughter Rino some really good food!" he added.

"Oh, come on! Can't you just be cool for once?" chided Shinichi as he playfully punched this massive helicopter parent on the shoulder.

It went without saying that the only pain was to the back of Shinichi's hand.

Chapter 4 

Talk and Money Make the World Go Round 

Thanks to the river flowing from Dog Valley, Boar Kingdom controlled large swaths of fertile land, ideal for agriculture. This made it a target for many neighboring countries. As a result, the city was surrounded with high walls, and the castle gates were guarded by many soldiers, harshly questioning and interrogating any suspicious individuals. Obviously, they weren't going to let a scruffy, middle-aged farmer walk in with a gorgeous, pale maid with blond locks.

"You there! Where'd you come from?"

"Oh yes, my name is Manju from the Daifuku village in the south. I'm here to find some work," replied the farmer.

"Daifuku? I've never heard that name before," said the guard, leering incredulously at the friendly farmer who was smiling from ear to ear. "And why's a backwater hick like you looking for work with a beauty like this?" He ogled the fair-haired maid from head to toe.

The farmer stooped in closer to the guard to interrupt his lewd stare.

"Yes, well, she's the most beautiful girl in our village, so she's been called to serve a noble household," he said, fishing out a few small pieces of glittering gold from his pouch and firmly pressing them into the guard's hand.

"So you've come to serve the nobility. Impressive." With a grin, the guard quickly slipped the gold into his breast pocket. His demeanor completely changed. "I'd also like the service of a woman this beautiful."

The guard knew she would've had a letter of introduction if she'd actually been invited to serve a noble household. Seeing she didn't, he knew their story was a lie and guessed she was probably being sold to a brothel.

"Yes, of course. Please come when you have the chance."

"I look forward to it. All right, on you go," prodded the guard with a vulgar smirk as he opened the path for the small-statured farmer and his companion.

The two passed through the gate, walking down the road before quickly ducking into the shadows between some buildings. At that moment, the *Illusion* spell melted off them, and the middle-aged farmer turned back into a high school boy.

"He didn't see through our magic and eagerly caved to a bribe. It seems the average soldier doesn't have much talent or interest in the job." Shinichi snickered.

"We did that little role-play so you could confirm *that*?" The blond maid questioned Shinichi, shrugging with some annoyance. The woman, of course, was Celes, but she continued holding her illusion, as her long ears would immediately give her away.

"Just in case. I wanted to get a feel for this country."

If they wanted to enter the city, they could've waited until nightfall and flown over the walls, but Shinichi insisted on walking through the gate in order to investigate.

"It isn't safe to make assumptions based on a sample size of one, but the gatekeeper didn't seem afraid of execution for accepting a bribe. Their laws probably aren't super-strict and stuff," he noted as he smiled wickedly.

From a criminal's point of view, he was thankful for this. He patted the heavy pouch swinging at his waist and filled with gold pieces.

"The King gave us access to his mountain of gold, to use it all if need be. It didn't work with the knight and his party, but it may well win over or settle things with the nobility and merchants," he continued.

"Settle things with money? Human culture is completely incomprehensible," said Celes, cocking her head in utter confusion. Shinichi had assumed this method was universally applicable.

"Huh, I figured you also had a monetary system in the demon world, I mean, you collect gold, for crying out loud."

"Yes, but we usually barter and trade."

"So you never pay money to avoid wars or bribe the enemy's general?"

"Why would we do something like that? One should just aim to win those fights. If you lose, isn't it your fault for being weak?"

"Ah yes, you're completely right," he said, looking at Celes, as she pursued her peculiar logic. He decided to give up trying to explain it to her.

If their culture's so advanced they build castles and use cutlery, why are they such muscle heads…?

Shinichi guessed it might have something to do with magic.

Come to think of it, armed with the knowledge of fire, monkeys evolved into humans precisely because they were weak. They weren't like bears with their incredible strength and claws. They didn't have fast reflexes or the fangs of tigers. And they definitely didn't have the massive bodies of elephants. In order to survive in this cruel world, they were forced to forge a weapon no other animal possessed: intellect.

They learned to sharpen rocks into weapons, coordinate attacks with their companions, and lure enemies into pitfalls. All because they were weak. If they had the strength to defeat bears and tigers with their bare hands, monkeys would've never evolved into humans, and they would all still be living freely and easily in the forest.

But demons were born with magic, a power far greater than claws or fangs. This was why every situation was settled with it, and it definitely wasn't coincidence they'd think every problem could be solved by their magical prowess.

If that's the case, I'm not sure why the demons were able to develop intellect on par with humans. Even though there were so many physical differences among them, they all seem to share a base level of intelligence. Should I just chalk that up as a coincidence, too?

It'd be easier to believe a higher being created them.

"What's our plan from here?" asked Celes, pulling Shinichi out of his thoughts.

"Well, first, let's gather some more information," replied Shinichi, walking down the street again.

"Information? Do you intend to find the hero's location?" Celes called after him.

"That's one piece of information, but food first."

"...What?"

Shinichi ignored the maid's exasperated voice and walked down the street in search of a suitable store.

"All right. Let's go with this one," he said as he opened the door of a building that appeared, based on the sign out front with a beer keg on it, to be a tavern.

Inside, there were four old, well-polished, round wooden tables in a neat row and a grim, middle-aged owner standing at the front counter, cutting some potato-like vegetables.

"Welcome. Please take a seat at the counter," he invited.

It seemed they'd just opened, as they were the only customers. Taking a seat at the counter as directed, Shinichi placed three pieces of gold in front of him as he ordered.

"Two of your shop's most expensive and delicious meals, please," he said.

"You idiot! Everything we serve is delicious." The owner seemed perturbed by Shinichi's cocky order, but he smiled as he took the gold. "You don't have any silver coins? What boonies did you come from?"

"From the Senbei village in the south," replied Shinichi.

"Hmm, that's the first I've ever heard of it," said the owner, making small talk as he pulled about twenty thin silver coins from his cashbox and placed them in front of Shinichi. "Your change. The currency exchange shop's right down this road toward the castle. It's the shop with scales on the sign."

"Ah, okay. Thanks." Sincerely grateful, Shinichi placed the silver coins in his pouch. He wasn't sure he'd been given the correct change, but the owner didn't seem like a bad guy, seeing as he'd given them some money back. He'd even told them about the currency exchange shop.

"So has there been anything interesting going on lately?" asked Shinichi.

"Not really. Let's see. Those legendary demons showed up in Dog Valley. Oh, and we lost horribly against them. Everywhere you look, we only have bad news." The owner sighed as he placed wooden cups filled with a pale brown liquid in front of Shinichi and Celes.

Is this ale? I've heard in ancient Europe, they drank alcohol because it didn't carry parasites, unlike water.

It was admittedly a bit too late, but he started worrying whether the water at the Demon King's castle had been safe to drink. Never mind that. Sipping his glass of ale, he chose to forget the legal drinking age. Celes watched him and followed suit. When she took her first sip, her eyes opened wide at its bursting flavor profile, and she pressed her hand over her mouth.

Just as I expected. Alcohol in the demon world must be pretty horrible, too.

He remembered he'd consumed a tiny amount of ale in the human world. It didn't exactly taste that great. And when he was a kid, his uncle let him drink a bit of alcohol just for fun. This was the extent of his experience, and though he couldn't be certain, he still felt this ale tasted like really watered-down Japanese beer.

It's either the ingredients or his cooking skills. If this continues, then the food must be...

"I'm warming up the soup, but eat this in the meantime. Here ya go," said the owner, plunking down a plate with thinly sliced ham and black bread.

"Thanks," replied Shinichi, lowering his expectations as he lifted the ham and bread to his mouth.

Hmm. The ham's a bit salty but not too bad. This bread, though... It's hard and sour.

It wasn't like the white loaves sold in Japan and tasted similar to rye bread in Germany. Flour in the twenty-first century was far superior to this bitter wheat grain.

Thank you, selective plant breeding.

As he thought, Shinichi looked to his side at Celes, whose eyes opened wider out of wonderment and delight. Their reactions couldn't have been more different.

"It's delicious…," she said, her stony face giving way to a rare sight—a slight smile. "So *this* is the bread Lady Rino spoke of and properly cooked meat. I never thought it'd be this wonderful."

These dishes were real, authentic cuisine from the human world, completely different from the unrefined food at the banquet. Celes's eyes sparkled like a child's as she furiously stuffed the morsels into her small mouth. Shinichi caught himself staring at her uncharacteristically childlike mannerisms and slid the plate with his leftovers in front of her.

"You can have the rest if you'd like. It's a bit salty for me," he said.

"Lord Shinichi… There's no use trying to dose me with an aphrodisiac. I'll never sleep with you," she insisted.

"I'm not dosing you! I don't have any!"

Though she was hell-bent on treating him like a pervert and accusing him of wrongdoing, she went ahead and ate his bread and ham without reservation.

Afterward, the owner handed them some soup with potatoes (or some similar vegetable), simply seasoned with salt but definitely edible. For the first time since coming into this world, Shinichi was satiated. He smiled and went back to the task at hand.

"By the way, I heard there's a hero who's come to beat the demons you were just talking about," he said to the owner.

"Hero? Oh yeah, you're talking about that young maiden Arian. If I'm not mistaken, she's actually staying here at my inn," he replied.

"…Hmm, is that so?" Shinichi swallowed his surprise. He looked beyond the owner's extended finger, pointing at the sleeping quarters on the second floor.

I'd heard she was in the city, but to think she'd actually be at this shop…

Though it was a simple coincidence, Shinichi's mind was so corrupt it made him suspicious this was some kind of trap.

"This hero, Arian, is she really that strong?" he asked.

"Aye, I haven't seen it with my own eyes, mind you, but I hear she's got the strength of a beast. We've had some other heroes, and she single-handedly beat 'em all at once."

"Oh, that's impressive."

He knew she'd been able to injure the Demon King, so it was obvious she was more powerful than those five heroes, all of whom failed to leave a single scratch. Shinichi considered this as he tried to change topics as naturally as possible.

"The Goddess's heroes…if they're that incredible, I wonder if I could be one."

"……"

Fearing he might be contemplating betraying them, Celes silently sharpened her gaze. But he wasn't thinking about that at all. The owner let out a loud guffaw as if to blow away the chilled air between his two customers.

"Don't be stupid. If a scrawny kid like you could be a hero, then I could become a hero, too!" he said.

"Ha-ha, yeah. You got me there." Shinichi smirked.

"There are fifty thousand people in Boar Kingdom, but legend has it that only six…no, seven people have been chosen by the Goddess to serve as heroes. Are you that good at sword fighting or magic?"

"Nah, there's no way. Guess I should just give it up," said Shinichi with a warm grin that matched the owner's. On the inside, his smile was much more sinister.

So there's seven people. If you take out the knight and his party of four, that leaves us with Arian and one other.

He'd also learned the heroes weren't chosen by blood or heritage but for being the strongest. There was only one other thing he wanted to check.

"Hey, is it true that if you become one of the heroes, you can be resurrected without a corpse?"

This wasn't just an inference; it was a wish. If every single person could be resurrected from nothing, the demons had no chance of winning. Shinichi waited nervously for his answer, and the owner nodded with a wry smile.

"Yeah, well, it sounds nice to be resurrected in any condition or circumstance. But normal folk like us don't really die in horrible ways anyway," replied the owner.

"Mm, yeah, it'd have to be pretty terrible if your body sustained so much damage it was incapable of resurrection… I guess it could happen if you're incinerated or something."

"Or if a hunter gets swallowed whole by a giant snake, digesting you to your bones."

"Blech. You'd be pretty traumatized even if you *could* come back to life."

"I mean, there are the poor, who're told they didn't donate enough to the church to receive the spell. It's a luxury to be resurrected with no strings attached," mused the owner.

"I see." Shinichi nodded in agreement, but he was dancing in victory on the inside.

All right! Their normal conditions for resurrection are about the same as the demons. The heroes are just a special case.

Shinichi didn't know the reason behind this, but the Goddess sure seemed miserly, only saving her chosen few. Thanks to that, though, he only needed to worry about the heroes.

"By the way, if I visited the cathedral without any money, would they be all, like, *Heathen, get out!* and chase me away?" asked Shinichi.

"…Is the priest in your village that cruel?"

"Ah, um, no? It's just the city's such a scary place, so I wasn't sure if the priests were also kind of stingy or something," Shinichi responded hastily. He'd asked out of curiosity, but the owner expressed such pity for him that Shinichi found himself backpedaling. "Our priests aren't that miserly. In fact, they'll even wait for you to pay your donations. But a debt's a debt. It looks bad if you never pay, so if you're some old guy out of a job, there's not much you can do…"

"Well, that can't be helped." To the owner's strangely vague reply, Shinichi looked back at him quizzically before nodding.

Guess resurrecting the dead certainly has its own problems, huh?

Just imagining the aftermath of resurrecting some people was terrifying, like a woman who'd been killed by her husband for committing adultery. If he'd had more time, Shinichi would've been interested in learning more about their laws and population issues.

"Thank you, sir. We'll definitely come back sometime," Shinichi promised, rising from his seat. He was thankful from the bottom of his heart for hearing such useful information. Celes followed him, and they placed their hands on the door to leave.

At that exact moment, an energetic call echoed down from the second floor of the tavern.

"Good morning, sir!"

"Ah, morning, miss. You're up later than usual today," greeted the owner.

"Yeah, I was up all night training and accidentally overslept!" said the redheaded girl as she bounded down the stairs to take a seat at the counter. The scarf on her neck was the same color as her hair and served as a symbol of justice. She seemed energetic and honest, and she walked in the path of light, a far cry from a certain someone and his twisted personality.

This was the Goddess's hero, the only person who'd been able to injure the Demon King.

"She really is just a girl…," observed Shinichi. He'd only seen her for a moment, but he was unable to conceal his surprise at her physique, even after hearing the King's story about their fight.

"Is it that strange she's a girl?" Celes asked.

"No, that's not it."

In this world, magic eliminated any semblance of a gender gap. One look at Celes was proof enough. No, the thing that caught his attention was much simpler, more pedestrian.

"It's just I thought she was kind of cute," he admitted.

"And it'd be fun to get her all wet with her tears and an unnamed white substance? You're a pervert."

"What? Do I really look like a sex offender?"

What's with her perpetual need to put people down and her sexual innuendoes? This was perhaps a greater mystery than the unexplainable methods the heroes used to respawn.

After leaving the tavern, Shinichi and Celes asked for directions from passersby to find their way to the center of the city, where the castle stood. Right next to it, there was a massive stone building, overloaded with garish decorations. This was a place of worship for a certain being who'd come up in their conversation earlier and was the greatest threat to the Demon King.

"Welcome, travelers. What brings you to the Boar Kingdom Cathedral of Our Goddess Elazonia?" A middle-aged woman who greeted Shinichi and Celes was wrapped in a pure-white robe with a golden symbol and appeared to be a member of the clergy. She spoke with a gentle smile that seemed tired at the same time.

A church dedicated to the Goddess who chose the heroes. All right, let's see what's going on.

Shinichi spoke with a perfectly natural smile on his face, despite the fact they were about to infiltrate the home base of their enemy.

"I'm from the Senbei village in the south, and I thought that I'd like to offer my prayers to our Goddess in this magnificent Boar Kingdom Cathedral."

"Oh, what a wonderful idea. Things are somewhat hectic right now, but please come on in," the woman offered. The two followed her lead, passed through the door, and set foot in the Goddess's cathedral.

Inside, its complex and beautiful construction featured many arches, and made of finely polished marble, its floors and pillars had a certain grandeur.

"It looks like they're doing pretty well for themselves. Maybe I should found a religion to make some money, too."

"*That's* your only impression?"

Shinichi and Celes spoke in quiet whispers so the priestess walking in front of them couldn't hear, but suddenly, Shinichi saw something that interested him.

"This is..."

There was a massive painting on the wall depicting a horned demon sitting astride a sinister black dragon, both falling into a bottomless abyss in a terrifying and hellish scene.

"This painting shows the defeat of the Evil God and Evil Dragon, cast into the bowels of the world long ago by the almighty powers of the good gods in an effort led by our Divine Goddess," the priestess kindly explained, but there was a shadow of fear and anger on her face. "Sometimes, I think about how terrifying it is that there are such evil beings sealed below the land we walk on," she continued.

"I agree," said Shinichi, responding appropriately and then asking a quick question. "I can understand how the Evil God might be feared, but is the dragon really that evil?"

He wasn't particularly surprised about dragons in this world. After all, they were in a fantastical world where magic existed. Even though the massive beasts tended to have a reputation for evil on Earth, there were many legends of good dragons in Asia and the Middle East, such as the Azure Dragon of the Four Symbols. He also vaguely remembered hearing that certain types with colors in their names, like the Red Dragon, were evil, but those associated with the color gold were good.

This was the train of thought going through his head when he asked his question, not really meaning anything more by it, but the woman's eyes opened in surprise and suspicion given he was a foreigner.

"It's been said that the dragons ate and killed all the gods other than our Divine Goddess, Elazonia. They are truly evil existences. Our Goddess will punish you if you're ever foolish enough to think there are such things as good dragons," she warned.

"Of course. I'm sorry." Shinichi did his best to seem apologetic after being told off, as a child might for acting mischievously. He then cast a glance at Celes next to him.

"Is what she said true?" he whispered.

"...It's completely different from the tales we're taught as demons." The maid's face looked slightly upset as she replied. "We have no idea how long it's been there or where it came from, but demons do talk about a Black Dragon sleeping in the depths of the demon world."

She also explained they regarded the dragon as a powerful and noble being, though not necessarily "good" if measured by the human concept of good and evil.

"Let me tell you about one legend. Some time ago, there was a demon who called himself the Black Demon King. As a result of his own hubristic desire to be the only black creature, he led a massive army against the Black Dragon."

"I feel like I can see where this is going." Shinichi moaned.

Celes shook her head at Shinichi, who'd hastily concluded the whole army had been eliminated.

"No, he and his entire army were said to have returned without a single casualty. However, he gave up his title as the Black Demon King, and upon hearing this, not a single demon took up the name Black ever again."

"Why?" Shinichi thought about the Blue Demon King. Having a title associated with a color must be quite an honor for demons. When Celes continued her explanation, it was quite obvious why the Black Demon King had given up his name.

"His entire army put everything they had into attacking the Black Dragon, but they failed to tear off a single scale, much less wake the dragon from its slumber."

"What?!" Shinichi accidentally exclaimed, making the priestess eye him suspiciously. He tried to brush it off with vague smile. "So you're telling me this self-professed Demon King's will was broken just by being treated like a pest?"

"The story's been passed down as a lesson to humbly keep improving oneself, so there's no proof it's true."

Even so, many demons believed the Black Dragon existed, and they worshipped and aspired to such absolute power.

"And our own Demon King?" he asked.

"He reveres the Black Dragon and said he'd like to go search for it once Lady Rino has grown up and leaves his side."

"I seriously can't imagine him ever leaving Rino given how he acts." Shinichi poked fun at him, but he couldn't help but be nervous deep inside.

Hmm, dragons, huh...? In recent releases, there've been games where you'd hunt them for their scales and claws, but I'm guessing that's not the case here.

Dubious about its existence, he took it as a good thing that there was no chance he'd be meeting this legendary being. He wanted to ask for more specifics about the dragon but was worried they might seem suspicious if their conversation went on any longer, and the two walked away from the painting.

Almost immediately, something else caught Shinichi's eye: At the end of a very broad aisle, there were rows of armored figures. There were several hundreds of them, and each one had a clean hole in its chest. They were the soldiers' corpses.

"Those can't possibly be...," began Shinichi.

"Yes, these are the royal soldiers who gave their lives in a brave fight against the evil Demon King," confirmed the woman, bowing deeply to show her respect for their service, though she expressed visible bitterness toward the demons. "Thanks to our Goddess's protection, their bodies will all be resurrected, but there's just too many victims. We've tried everything—half of them were taken to churches nearby—but it's just too much for the bishop to handle..."

A spell had been cast to keep the corpses from decomposing as they waited for resurrection.

"I've tried to help out where I can, but considering the Bishop's other duties, we can only save fifty people per day...," she continued.

"I see. Thank you for your service." Shinichi's expression was somber, but he was gleeful to glean more information.

So they don't have many people capable of casting the Resurrection *spell.*

On the demons' side, the King and Celes were the only two who could cast these spells, though Rino might be able to with great effort.

They'd have some serious problems if the humans had spell casters like them all over the place.

They're relatively weak, but it seems they can help each other out. I wonder if they can lend their MP to others or divide their powers. One particular battle manga comes to mind.

Either way, they shouldn't take the humans lightly or look down on their potential.

The trio finally reached the prayer room at the end of the cathedral, as Shinichi was still deep in thought. The prayer room, taller and wider than any of the others, didn't contain any corpses. Instead, the light filtered through the glass windows to illuminate the only thing present—a saintly white statue of a woman.

"So this is the Goddess…," remarked Shinichi.

She was a beautiful woman with long hair and a serene smile, but she had no wings and resembled a human in physique.

Shinichi and Celes pretended to give their appropriate prayers by taking cues from another family praying in the chamber. Afterward, Shinichi asked Celes for a handkerchief, which he used to wrap up a large amount of gold to place in the hands of the priestess.

"Thank you for taking the time out of your busy day to help us. We don't know the ways of the city," he said, "but I would like to give this to the Goddess…"

"Oh, that's not necessary," objected the priestess.

"Please. We've been able to live peacefully thanks to the blessings of our Divine Goddess. It's the least I can do."

"Well, if you insist…" She accepted the gold after he repeatedly insisted she take it.

"You're really good at imitating plebeians," whispered Celes.

"Hey, I know that's not a compliment."

Shinichi let her sarcastic comment go before making a face as if he'd suddenly remembered something.

"By the way, I was wondering if I might be able to ask you a question," he said to the priestess.

"Of course. What is it?" she replied.

"My youngest brother's heard those stories about the demons lately, and he's gotten himself all worked up, saying things like, 'I'm going to become the Goddess's hero and beat them all!'"

"Oh, he sounds like an energetic little boy," said the priestess.

"It'd be too dangerous for him, so we don't plan on letting him do it, but I was wondering if I could ask you a little about the heroes."

"I can definitely do that much."

Having accepted a large amount of gold from them, the priestess happily invited them to take a seat in some chairs against the wall.

"First of all, how are the heroes chosen?" asked Shinichi.

"First, they must excel in either the martial or magical arts, and they must also have the courage and strength to defeat the monsters who threaten humanity. Once they receive the Goddess's blessing, they're accepted as a hero for the first time."

Shinichi noticed the priestess used the word *monsters* instead of *demons*, but he continued asking about the heroes for now.

"I see. What's this blessing like?"

"It's nothing difficult. Those who are confident in their courage and strength stand in front of the statue of the Goddess in the church, offer themselves to her, and vow to fight for the people," explained the priestess.

"That's it?" Shinichi sounded incredulous.

"Yes, and if you're accepted by the Goddess, proof of your status as a hero will appear somewhere on your body." She pointed to the symbol of the Goddess depicted on her own robe.

"That's really all there is to it? I mean, if that's the case, I'd think there'd be far more heroes," said Shinichi.

His point left the priestess looking slightly confused.

"Well, if the criteria was only mastery of swordsmanship or magic, there'd probably be many more people capable of becoming heroes, but when you think about the courage and purity needed in order to be chosen..."

"Are you saying some people are skilled enough and still not chosen by her?" asked Shinichi.

He reworded his initial question, sensing it was difficult for her to answer, and the priestess leaned in to prevent others from overhearing.

"Being chosen as a hero is one of the greatest honors. Those aspiring for high positions in the church, like a cardinal or archbishop, must receive the Goddess's blessing. But if they aren't chosen… You know where this is going, right?" she asked.

There were many people who didn't seek the Goddess's blessing out of fear they might be labeled as impure and talked about behind their backs. It'd be a particularly hard blow for those in positions of power or those vulnerable to rumors, such as the royal family. It would also close off possibilities for future advancement for priests, as it would serve as proof she had rejected them. In the worst-case scenario, they'd be forced to leave the church—a death sentence, in essence. These risks would explain why more people didn't aim to become heroes, despite the obvious benefit of resurrection without limitations.

Would it be like being excommunicated from the church? I guess that'd be scary…

When someone volunteered themselves as a hero, they theoretically had the necessary skills and resulting achievements. Yet, they could be branded as "virtueless" in seconds and lose everything they'd worked for, which was a huge gamble with pretty poor odds.

The knight and his party must have been high rollers.

Though now, that knight was on the brink of destruction with no future prospects or a way to receive his title as an earl.

While Shinichi was deep in thought, Celes let out a huge sigh of relief next to him.

"I'm relieved you have no chance of becoming a hero and betraying us."

"Yeah, yeah, I'm a twisted bastard. Whatever." By this point, Shinichi was used to letting Celes's spiteful comments go and stood from his chair.

"Thank you for speaking with us. One last thing: This might be rude of me to ask but…does the Goddess really look like that statue?"

"Excuse me?" For a moment, the priestess seemed at a loss for words, staring back with a blank look on her face, but she regained her composure and smiled. "Unfortunately, I haven't been blessed with the opportunity to see our Divine Goddess, so I can't say for sure."

"Oh, I see."

"However, the statue in the Archbasilica, which serves as a model for all other statues of the Goddess, was carved by the first pope, who's said to have been taught directly by the Goddess."

"I see. What a beautiful story. I'll share it with the other villagers." When Shinichi finished expressing his thanks, he turned his back on the priestess and the statue to leave.

As the two made to depart the church, a man in his thirties walked up to them with a crowd of clergymen in tow. His robes were simple but more impressive than others in the church. He raised his hand and smiled to devotees who bowed their heads as he passed by. Shinichi followed their lead, shuffling to the side to leave the aisle open and bowing his head in a position that would let him hide Celes. The man didn't seem to notice the maid in the shadows and walked by them as he continued to smile genially.

Hmm...

Shinichi saw something just before the man walked past him. Inside his right palm, there was the golden symbol of the Goddess.

So he must be the seventh hero and the highest-ranking church member here.

It was somewhat inconvenient that the last hero was also someone who could use the *Resurrection* spell, but it seemed he had neither the capacity to resurrect the remaining hundreds of dead soldiers nor the time to advance to the King's castle.

It seems our only real threat is that girl, Arian.

Shinichi continued calculating as he left the church and looked up at the blue sky.

"Were you able to extract the information you needed?" asked Celes.

"About seventy percent of it." Shinichi answered Celes's question half-heartedly and continued his musings.

I'd hoped to see a Goddess's hero get resurrected, but I guess that's asking for too much.

Though he delighted in his twisted fantasy of torturing the knight's party to reveal more information or conducting human experimentations on them, his expression started to cloud over.

I would've seemed too suspicious if I'd asked that priestess how the heroes are resurrected. Then again, she probably would've said something cheesy like "by the Goddess's power."

It's possible that no one—not the priestess or the other members of clergy, not a single other human being—knew the truth besides the Goddess and Her heroes.

I don't know if this Goddess Elazonia is a single intelligent being or a larger formless system in place, but one thing I do know is that someone or something exists.

Nobody had met the Goddess. But the heroes were capable of resurrection. And—

The Goddess can do something the King can't. She can bring people back to life from nothing. Does that mean she's more powerful than he is?

Scared by his own suspicions, Shinichi clenched his jaw to keep himself from trembling. He didn't even know exactly how powerful the King was, except that he was as powerful as a small-scale weapon of mass destruction. He had more than enough power to cause wide-scale devastation. Could there be a deity that could surpass him?

If you're out there, please don't reveal yourself.

At this point, there didn't seem to be any chance of the Goddess appearing, but what would happen if a situation arose where humanity teetered on the brink of annihilation?

I need to make sure things don't get out of hand for the sake of the humans and the demons.

Sometime earlier, Rino had told him that if the humans attacked the demon world, the demons would annihilate humankind in retaliation, but it might just be that the demons would be the ones to find themselves on the brink of total destruction.

"What do we do next?" asked Celes.

"Uh, yeah." Shaken from his thoughts, Shinichi focused on the task at hand. He tried to speak optimistically. "We have a haiku where I'm from: A computer is / nothing more than just a box / if the OS breaks."

"Huh…?"

"To put it in simpler terms, everything's over when you sever the head issuing the orders," he said, making a perfunctory effort to reword the saying as he turned his gaze to the large castle next to the church. "In other words, let's overthrow their king."

Presumably, it was their king giving the orders to attack the demons. There'd be no need to fight the heroes if they defeated the ruler of Boar Kingdom.

"We can win without fighting. This is the most basic strategy of war," he said.

"You put all this effort into investigating the heroes to reach this conclusion?" asked Celes.

"It's *because* I investigated them. It's pointless to take on the heroes if we can't get rid of whatever trick they're using to resurrect," replied Shinichi.

If all went according to plan, it wouldn't matter if more heroes came along if they kept the King in check and could preserve the peace at the Demon King's castle.

"But can we defeat their king?" Celes sounded concerned. To the basic mind-set of a demon, it was natural to think the king was the most powerful being, but Shinichi nodded to reassure her.

"It'll be fine. It's not like we're going to get into a fistfight."

"What?"

"A fight between politicians can be settled with talk and *this* right here." Shinichi slipped a silver coin out of the heavy pouch hanging at his hip. "You can do anything as long as you have money. Long live capitalism!"

"That's so dirty," said Celes coldly. She might not have known anything about human society, but she knew this as a fact.

Every morning, Tortoise IV began his daily duties by making an appearance in front of an audience. He met with the lower-ranking nobility, the guilds that supported the city's economy, and ambassadors from other countries. He listened to their suggestions and requests and provided answers after consulting with his ministers.

He always thought it'd be faster to get rid of this stiflingly formal affair and deal with their issues by letter, but part of his duty was to act with a particular degree of pomp and circumstance in front of them.

Not that a puppet of the church has a say in anything.

Inside his mind, Tortoise IV let out a heavy sigh and held on to his last shred of self-respect as he took his seat on the throne with performative regal grace.

"Who do we have first today?" he asked.

"Yes. About that...," said the prime minister, looking puzzled at the parchment in his hand. "It seems to be a merchant called Manju from the Daifuku village."

"A village merchant? If it's about trade, he should contact the guild."

The king wasn't so idle that he had time to meet one-on-one with merchants.

The minister knew that, of course, but pressed on. "Yes, but to express his desire to meet directly with Your Highness, he sent this..." Blinking rapidly, he signaled two guards to carry a large chest forward. They set the chest down in front of the king with a heavy thump and gently opened the lid.

The gold inside reflected an immense light, filling the audience chamber and momentarily dazzling everyone.

"What?! The chest's filled with gold bars?!" exclaimed the king.

"The contents have been tested. It's all pure gold—no other metals mixed in."

Converted to the country's currency, its contents were the equivalent of over one hundred thousand gold coins. Considering the yearly pay of a solider was fifteen gold coins, it was an absurdly large amount of money.

"He said he gives it as a gift in hopes of your appearance, regardless of your answer."

"Absurd! Who exactly is this person?!"

The king's surprise was not without reason. The guild leaders and ambassadors had offered gifts to appease him in the past, but their combined monetary worth wouldn't even make up one hundredth of what was within this chest. It was customary for the value to be in proportion to the request, but this merchant called Manju had just given a mountain of gold to meet with the king.

"He can't possibly be some village merchant. Who is he? Where is he actually from?" inquired the king.

"Nobody in the Merchants' Guild has heard of him..."

Merchants were known to receive information faster than nobles and knights. If they didn't know who he was, then no one in Boar Kingdom did.

"Your Highness, what shall we do?"

"Hmmm..." Tortoise IV groaned, deep in thought.

This merchant was obviously suspicious, likely an agent from one of the other countries aiming to take over Boar Kingdom. Despite this, the king was tempted to devour this forbidden fruit, even while knowing it was poisonous. In front of him, the gold glittered and winked as if to guarantee there was more where this came from. Boar Kingdom was not so rich that he could reject such an offer without at least considering it first.

If only half our treasury hadn't been drained out by our attempts to resurrect the fallen soldiers...

The country had made large donations to the church in order to cover the costs of resurrecting the soldiers who had fallen at the hands of the Demon King. Half the soldiers needed to be taken to churches in neighboring countries, which meant the king needed to prepare dozens of horse-drawn carriages. For some reason, he was burdened with this responsibility, though Bishop Hube had originally insisted—no, forced him—to deploy the troops.

To take it one step further, he was starting to suspect the church might have waged war on the demons in order to receive more donations and weaken the power of his kingdom.

Is this merchant one of the church's pawns?

Tortoise IV glanced furtively at Bishop Hube, standing next to him and looking at the gold with unchanging serenity.

"Bring him in," ordered the king.

He wouldn't know if it was a trap or who sent him until he met the man.

Obeying his request, the minister brought the merchant to stand in front of his throne. Wearing modest clothing, he was a middle-aged man of average build, average height, and no distinguishing features. Behind him, however, was a blue-haired maid so beautiful that gazing upon her felt like looking at the world for the first time.

"Your Excellency, King Tortoise IV, I'm truly honored to be in your presence," said the merchant.

"It's my pleasure. Raise your head," said the king, responding with routine formality. The merchant had respectfully taken a knee and slipped his head into a bow. "Well, what did you wish to speak about?"

"Yes, I wish to request Your Highness's permission to open trade," stated the merchant.

"Trade? If that's the case, would it not be faster to discuss this with the Merchants' Guild?"

If he approached them with that amount of money, the guild would certainly welcome him with open arms. However, the middle-aged merchant Manju gently shook his head.

"Unfortunately, I cannot begin this trade without Your Highness's approval."

"I don't understand. What exactly is it that you wish to do?"

The man answered with a tiny, evil smirk after confirming he'd grabbed the monarch's attention.

"I wish to open trade with the demons in Dog Valley."

"Wh-what?!"

The king, the minister, the ambassadors, and even the guards were all shocked by the merchant's words. Even Bishop Hube opened his eyes wide in surprise.

"Are you insane? Are you seriously asking to open trade with the demons?!" cried the king.

"I'm perfectly sane. But sanity isn't what makes a merchant successful," he replied, flashing a fearless smile to the flustered Tortoise IV. "I've already heard the rumors that the demons are horrifying. However, I question whether or not they're truly our enemies."

"Wh-what do you mean?!"

The king's shoulders unconsciously shook, suggesting the same exact thought had crossed his mind. Seeing this, the merchant seemed satisfied and continued.

"Though they faced six thousand soldiers and killed half of them, the demons haven't made further advances against Boar Kingdom, right? If they're truly as powerful as rumored, they probably could take the country in three days if they tried."

"Mm-hmm..."

"And if all that's true, there's only one explanation. The demons in Dog Valley don't see us as an enemy. At the very least, it means they have no desire to destroy Boar Kingdom."

"Wha—?!"

Though Tortoise IV raised his voice in surprise, he was convinced because he'd already come to the same conclusions earlier. This, however, wasn't something that could be taken lightly.

"We're talking about the evil demons, the kin of the Evil God who was defeated by the Gods and driven to the depths of the earth. It's only expected they find us, the children of the Gods, abhorrent!" Tortoise IV deflected the merchant's argument by referencing this well-known folklore. He held it in front of him like a shield.

However, the mysterious man simply shook his head slowly, seemingly unfazed.

"Perhaps the legends were wrong. Well, maybe the demons are evil beings. But just as humans are rarely born evil, perhaps the demons in Dog Valley are friendly."

"That can't possibly be..."

"They executed a controlled attack, killing only half of the six thousand soldiers in such a way that they could be resurrected. They've been attacked from all sides yet haven't retaliated. Instead, they remain in the valley as recluses... Do you not see these facts alone are enough to make this explanation seem reasonable?"

"......"

Tortoise IV was silent, faced with the reality of their situation, far away from vague legends and folklore.

Could it be true? Could these demons not be as evil as the legends say?

Had they simply been blinded by fear of the Demon King thrashing their army and his extreme strength? If he cast aside his prejudices and assumptions, the merchant's explanation certainly seemed plausible.

"I mean, even though they haven't advanced into our territory, they killed a large number of the kingdom's soldiers and drove away the heroes. Obviously, we can't trust them so easily. Maybe they have some hidden motive as to why they haven't attacked us yet," continued the merchant.

"Hmm."

"This is why I'd like to make first contact with the demons through the guise of trade and attempt to learn their true intentions."

"Hmm..."

There was some truth in the merchant's words. The king had nothing to lose from this plan.

"But what's in it for you?" he asked, and the merchant flashed another sinister smile.

"If I'm able to successfully open trade with the demons, I'll obtain items and skills known only to them. I imagine that'd be worth a fortune hundreds of times more than what I've given you."

"Yes, but that doesn't necessarily mean they'll give you what you seek," rebuffed the king.

"Trading's a gamble. It's necessary to accept the risk of failure. Even if there are no goods or skills, there's sure to be one thing even more valuable."

"And what's that?"

He smirked wickedly at the deeply interested king hanging on the edge of his seat.

"A connection to insurmountable strength, the power to win against armies of tens of thousands of soldiers—a connection to the Demon King."

"What—?!"

Everyone in the audience chamber was stunned by the answer. What the merchant was suggesting was dangerous and sacrilegious yet so incredibly tempting.

"If the Demon King became our ally, you could destroy and conquer other countries. Boar Kingdom could become one large, unified kingdom. Do you not dream of creating the Boar Empire?"

"The Boar Empire… I could be an emperor…?" he speculated, stunned.

"Even if it doesn't go that well, you could still form an alliance with the Demon King, putting a check on enemy countries and preventing them from attacking us. I'm not well educated in such matters, so I can't be certain, but have we not been attacked by other countries two or three times in the past?"

"Hmm…"

The merchant's words were as sweet and dangerous as nectar, and they ate away at Tortoise IV's heart.

"Say that I fail. All that you would've lost is one idiot merchant. Your Highness, please permit me to trade with the demons," pleaded the merchant, bringing his request to a close as he bowed his head once again.

His words were backed by reason. Boar Kingdom had nothing to lose and everything to gain. If it were up to him, the king would have no reason to consider this request further.

"I—I—"

Clap, clap, clap.

The king's response was interrupted by the sound of a dry clap.

The noise came from someone standing next to the king, a man with an unwaveringly saintly smile—the Goddess's bishop.

"A wonderful performance, you heretical merchant," he said.

"Heretical?" asked the man, his eyebrows raising in surprise.

Bishop Hube's smile deepened as if to suggest that much was obvious.

"To join hands with the enemy for money, to sleep with the vile demons who have wronged Elazonia, the Goddess of Light… If that's not stabbing our Goddess—no, all humanity—in the back, what is it?" accused Bishop Hube, casting his gaze at everyone in the audience chamber.

The look in his eyes said more than his words: If you went against the Goddess's teachings, you could kiss your life good-bye. For the

rest of your life, your wounds would go unmended, your illnesses left uncured, and worst of all, you wouldn't be brought back to life in the face of death.

And it went even deeper than that.

The church controlled the most powerful people in the world—the heroic immortals—and their swords would be pointed at your throat. They made the most horrifying assassins, coming after you again and again, no matter how many times you killed them.

There was no way the king would go against the Goddess if it meant sacrificing his life.

"Uh, um, yes, just as Bishop Hube says. I admire your enthusiasm for trade, but I cannot allow you to go against the Goddess's teachings," stammered the king.

"Absolutely. We don't have to rely on your filthy plan to go forward, as my prodigy, the hero Arian, will be eliminating the demons," asserted Bishop Hube. He cautioned him against stirring any unnecessary desires in the king, placing a hand on the ruler's shoulder.

"That's that. You should give up on your venture," said the minister, hoping the disquieting situation would be over soon.

"Your Highness and noble attendees, I sincerely apologize for wasting your time with such a foolish request. Please accept the gold as an apology," said the merchant. He brought their attention back to the gold in hopes they wouldn't question his indiscretions further.

"Hmm, you may speak with me again if you ever wish to begin trade elsewhere," said Tortoise IV in an apologetic tone, despite what the bishop had said.

The merchant gave a smile in response and turned to leave, but there was someone in the room who would not allow that.

"Guards, arrest the heretic," the Goddess's bishop demanded coldly despite his warm smile. "To turn your back on the Goddess and consort with the evil demons—he must be an agent of the cruel and hellish Demon King."

"Bishop Hube, you're going too far!" objected Tortoise IV, unintentionally raising his voice in response to the bishop's insubordination.

But the bishop's smile didn't waver.

"Your Highness, I'm absolutely certain this apostate is an agent of the Demon King. They're using magic to conceal their appearances."

"What?!"

Gasps of surprise filled the chamber again for what seemed like the hundredth time today, as everyone turned to look at the merchant and his maid. Both their faces hardened in response to the bishop's accusation.

"Now, agents of the evil Demon King, reveal your true selves. Or should I do it by my own hand?" he threatened as he menacingly raised his right hand with the symbol of the Goddess.

The maid had been silent until now, but she took a step forward when she saw the bishop attempt to use magic. The merchant, who was in charge, however, raised his hand to stop her.

"I'd hoped to conceal this, but if you so wish," he said, signaling to the maid with a look.

The maid complied with her master's request and broke the *Illusion* spell, which melted away from the merchant. And there he was—a figure with an ugly face covered in burn scars, indiscernible in age or any other facial features.

"Bleurgh..."

He started to speak again, ignoring the guard who'd just vomited.

"These scars were given to me by a rival merchant. I normally conceal them, as they're difficult for some to look upon."

"......"

"This girl also suffered similar scars, but please don't force her to reveal those," requested the merchant as he prostrated himself. He was unconcerned about his own image but desperate to spare the young girl from having to unveil her disfigured face in public.

The king and his ministers were not so cruel as to add insult to injury.

"Manju, raise your head. It is I who should apologize," spoke the king.

"I'm forever grateful for your kindness," said the man, lowering his head again, as the maid recast the *Illusion* spell and hid his scars, then turned to leave.

He stopped at the door to the audience chamber and turned back to speak.

"When I received these scars, I thought, *Humans are far more evil and horrifying than the monsters in our legends.* What do you think, bishop?" he asked, looking at Hube for a fleeting moment, then spinning and walking out the door without waiting for an answer.

The king let out a sigh of relief as the tension dissolved, and the bishop continued to look as genial as always. But—

"You think you can use your heretical charms to embarrass me? I'm a bishop of the Divine Goddess—!" cursed Hube in a voice so quiet no one else could hear.

For just that moment, his plastered grin faded to let his black heart bleed onto the surface of his face.

"Oh geez, looks like the 'Make a Contract with Me and Become Emperor' strategy was a big failure." Shinichi groaned, splayed on the bed at the inn, without too much apparent disappointment. He'd been wary someone was on his tail on their journey back.

Celes had returned to her brown-skinned, silver-haired self, and she quickly held her hands up to his face.

"If anyone has a right to say 'Oh geez,' it's me," insisted Celes, casting a *Healing* spell on the facial burns Shinichi had inflicted on himself.

"This came in handy, though, didn't it?"

He'd guessed they couldn't in good conscience make the demon maid remove her illusion if he showed horrendous scars on himself. He was right.

"Yes, but why are you willing to go this far?" asked Celes.

Everything had gone according to plan, and, obviously, they'd gotten rid of his ability to feel pain. Even from a demon's perspective, though, the act of burning one's own face was a bit too extreme.

"You're not only twisted and dirty minded but also an extremely masochistic pervert. Don't get carried away." She spat out her insults while looking unusually angry.

"Aw, Celes, were you worried about me?" mocked Shinichi.

"I worry about what goes on in your head," she retorted. As she talked, every scar on Shinichi's face completely vanished. "I also went ahead and connected your eyebrows for you. My treat."

"Do I *look* like a police officer from a certain nineties anime?! Anyway, we got what we needed," said Shinichi, rubbing between his eyebrows just in case. Smiling, he evaluated their performance again. "I think the king and his subordinates don't necessarily hate the demons and are willing to listen. The problem is that guy, Bishop Hube."

Shinichi was surprised someone they'd passed by in the church would interrupt their grand plan in the audience chamber, but thanks to that, they now knew their enemy.

"It seems the Goddess's followers and her heroes really hate demons. I mean, the knight and his party were the same. Do you know anything about this?" asked Shinichi.

"I do not. We do not hear talk about the Goddess in the demon world," replied Celes, shaking her head.

In the demon world, they didn't really learn about the legends of the Goddess sealing the Evil God and Evil Dragon in the depths of hell. Of course, they were troubled upon hearing the humans thought of them as the kin of the Evil God and, by extension, their enemy.

"Even if their stories are true, it has nothing to do with demons in the present day, right?"

"It's not very easy to convince humans with logic like that," replied Shinichi, letting out a heavy sigh. "Unfortunately for Rino, you can't really resolve religious malice and hate just by talking to one another."

Everyone knew faith was born out of emotions, not logic. Therefore, religious followers were more likely to fall into a thought pattern of believing something without reason or proof. Sometimes, they believed in something because it served them well. Other times, they might perceive something was correct just because they believed in it. They would then begin resisting other opinions. There were more than enough instances of zealots refusing to have a conversation in Shinichi's world.

"This means we're back to square one," said Shinichi. He'd have to use his intellect to force the heroes to stop attacking the Demon King's castle, returning to the original reason he'd been summoned to this world.

"That guy's voice, Bishop Hube's, changed a tiny bit when he said, 'My prodigy, the hero Arian.' I wonder what he'd think if she got caught in an R-rated situation with some demons, hee-hee-hee," he added.

"I have no idea what that means, but thanks for reminding me you're sick," sneered Celes, insulting Shinichi and his devious smile, though she made no effort to stop him. She'd lost any residual feelings of kindness toward the Goddess's followers, who refused to listen to others and arbitrarily decided they were evil. "Well? What do we do next?"

"Next up: training!" declared Shinichi without thinking.

"...Huh?" asked Celes, whose usually blank face looked a bit stupid.

Shinichi must have been truly sick and twisted for enjoying that view.

Chapter 5

Only Losers Talk Nonsense About Cowards

"It's time for Shinichi's three-minute training! Yay!" Shinichi yelled excitedly.

"Yay!" mimicked Rino happily.

"...What's this?" inquired Celes, abandoning her normally judgmental attitude.

To avoid suspicion, Shinichi and Celes had left the city as the merchant and his maid, casting the *Fly* spell in the middle of the night once they were on a southern road near Boar Kingdom. It was the day after their return to the Demon King's castle.

"Hey, Rino, is it all right for you to play here?" asked Shinichi.

"Yup! Daddy's busy with work, so it'd make me so very happy if I could play with you!"

"...A Demon King's work? Like paperwork and stuff?" Shinichi sounded skeptical.

"Paperwork? Um, you know Daddy's job is to beat up the bad guys and keep getting stronger, right?"

"Okay! You know what? That doesn't even surprise me anymore!" said Shinichi, forcing out an energetic laugh to fake some enthusiasm. "Actually, I'm going to do the same thing: train to get stronger. You think you could help me out, Rino?"

"You can count on me!"

"Why exactly are you suddenly interested in becoming stronger?" interrupted Celes sharply, finally returning to her senses.

"I'm preparing to defeat the heroes," replied Shinichi, also reverting to his normal self.

"So you fully admit you'll fail if you continue to be weak?"

"Yep. Also, I feel like I'll die outright if I don't train a bit," Shinichi admitted.

Since he was the Demon King's advisor, the King or Celes would probably bring him back using the *Resurrection* spell if he died. But if things kept escalating, someone was going to want him dead permanently. So a little preparation seemed important.

"Okay, but one day of training isn't going to change anything." Celes raised a valid concern.

Just as on Earth, the quickest path to strength was slow but intense regular training. But Shinichi was starting to learn rules could be bent with human intellect and magic.

"You'll see in a minute. Rino, can you cast the *Pain Block* spell?" Shinichi requested.

"Yes! It's the first type of magic we learn. Daddy says we must fight with all our strength till the moment before we die."

"Ah…um, sure. Could you cast that on me?"

"Yes! Mm!" said Rino as she puffed out her cheeks. Adorably calling upon her powers, she chanted, "Pain, pain, go away, come again another day! *Pain Block!*"

"Wait, that cute incantation was a *spell*?" asked Shinichi, thinking of the time Celes cast *Pain Block* so he could burn his face. She'd used a much simpler incantation.

"Yep, spells don't have any set incantations, so they're different depending on the caster," related Rino.

"I see," Shinichi said as a light sprang from Rino's palms and enveloped his body. He pinched his arms, and sure enough, he couldn't feel any pain. "All right, now for some high-speed strength training."

Shinichi placed both hands on the ground and started doing push-ups.

"One, two, three… This is amazing! I feel like I could go on forever."

Were he in his natural state, his chest and arms would go numb after twenty push-ups, and he'd reach his limit just before forty. But that number came and went. He couldn't feel anything but did, however, reach a physical limit where he just couldn't do any more.

"One hundred and two, one hundred and three... Augh, that might be it." Shinichi was unable to move his body no matter how hard he tried. He'd used all his strength doing push-ups. Collapsing on the ground, he pulled up his shirt to look at his pectoral muscles, red and swollen. He was bleeding internally after tearing a muscle by pushing it past its limits.

"Ah, that looks like it hurts." Rino winced.

"If I didn't have that spell on me, I probably would've died from the pain."

For a motivated athlete, this amount of training was entirely possible on Earth, but his next trick was only possible in a fantasy world.

"Rino, can you cast a spell to heal my torn muscles? I don't want a spell that'll turn back time or reconstruct my body or something. I want something that'll increase my natural healing process."

"Ah, um, I don't think I understand," stammered Rino, confused and shaking her head at Shinichi's complicated explanation.

Celes let out a heavy sigh and came over to sit down next to Shinichi.

"What if I improve your body's restorative capacity?" she suggested.

"Ah, that would be perfect."

"All right. *Self-Healing Power Boost!*" she said, casting the spell by placing her palms on Shinichi's swollen chest. A colorless energy flowed from Celes's hands and ran through his body. His chest was on fire as all the cells reproduced at an abnormally fast pace.

"Ooh, I can see it healing!"

The internal bleeding would've normally taken at least three days to heal, but it completely vanished in about a minute. That's not the only thing the magic did.

"Now we'll see if my idea works. One, two, three...," said Shinichi as he started doing push-ups again once his muscles were fully recovered.

And he kept going, even after he hit his previous limit of 103.

"One hundred and twenty, one hundred and twenty-one... I can still move! It worked!"

"What? Did you get stronger just by doing that?!" asked Rino in shock. Shinichi didn't stop his push-ups to explain in more detail.

"It's called post-workout recovery. Muscles get stronger because they repair themselves after their fibers are broken. Normally, you'd need to rest for like two or three days for it to fully heal, but I sped that process up with magic," explained Shinichi, reaching his new limit of one hundred fifty push-ups.

Celes cast the spell again, and Shinichi's muscles healed again, becoming stronger.

"It's not high-speed leveling up, it's high-speed strength training. Man, getting strong is fun!"

"You're cheating again. Do you ever feel bad for those who put in constant and steady effort?" asked Celes.

"Searching for the most efficient training method is its own kind of effort. It doesn't take much effort to stop thinking and do the same thing over and over again," replied Shinichi.

"And how do you really feel?"

"I love that I can cheat and take the easy way and still manage to do better than others!"

"You degenerate."

Shinichi started doing squats, enduring the insults to which he'd become accustomed.

"Rino, I'm sorry to ask you this, but could you run to get me some food and something to drink? I'll start to lose mass if I don't get enough nutrients, even with all this exercise and muscle restoration."

"Yep! I'll go prepare a feast for you!" beamed Rino, excited he was relying on her. She ran off toward the dining hall.

"Wow, she's such a good kid! Nothing like the Demon King at all."

"If you touch her—," warned Celes.

"Yeah, yeah, I know what'll happen. But that's beside the point—I won't do anything!"

"......"

"What's with that look? You know what? I know exactly what you're thinking: *That's something that a pedophile would say.*"

"That's something that a pedophile would say."

"So I was right? That's what you've been thinking all along?!" Shinichi's cry carried a bit more force than he'd intended, which broke them out of their normal comedic banter. Shinichi had a feeling the maid would enjoy *manzai*-style comedy.

"Okay, on a serious note, I think Rino's cute and all, but there's seriously no chance of anything romantic happening between us."

Though it was entirely possible Rino was actually older than Shinichi, as they were different species, it still was out of the question. He couldn't shake the moral standards of his home country.

"I don't have any siblings, so I just see her as a little sister. I want to spoil her, that's all."

"...As do I," agreed Celes, uncharacteristically responding in a serious tone. In fact, her face seemed a little softer. Her relationship with Rino was beyond that of a maid and her master's daughter, and she seemed to really care about her.

"Just to be clear, I'm more into big boobs, so I actually prefer busty women like you, Celes!" declared Shinichi, intentionally saying something rude to break out of this embarrassingly tender moment. He'd thought she'd call him out for sexual harassment or being a pervert, but—

"......" Celes said nothing, turning her face from Shinichi and looking down.

"Um, Celes?"

"......"

"Are you blushing, by chance?"

"Hyper Gravity!"

"Ah?!"

Shinichi's body suddenly became so heavy he was unable to remain standing and sprawled on the floor like he'd been nailed down.

"I am going to help Lady Rino. I will be back shortly," quipped Celes.

"No, wait—before you go! Could you undo...?"

"It's my gift to you. Good luck on your training." Celes smiled like a flower in full bloom as she left the room. Just before the doors closed, though, she looked back at Shinichi as if he were a pig awaiting slaughter.

"She's...surprisingly innocent..."

Shinichi found this glimpse of a cuter Celes somewhat endearing,

but the bones in his body were starting to make a horrendous creaking sound, and he prepared himself for his first death.

Rino had rushed to save Shinichi, who'd narrowly escaped death and resumed training. This was his third day.

"People used to call me a little weakling, but now I'm pretty buff!" Shinichi marveled, unable to resist flexing his muscles. He was stronger than the time he'd used questionable training gear.

"Wow! Amazing! You look just like Daddy!"

"Repulsive." Celes was spitting her normal venom in stark contrast to Rino, who was excitedly swinging from Shinichi's arm.

"Anyway, I think that's enough strength training for now," said Shinichi.

Doing much more would damage his health. Truth be told, it was more painful to keep eating all the food he needed to build muscle. It'd be different on Earth with its gourmet cuisine, but here he was eating lots of unfamiliar ingredients from the demon world: gamy meats and boiled weeds. It would have been less painful to undergo torture, which is why he wanted to focus his attention on the demons and their fantastical power.

"So how would I be able to use magic?" asked Shinichi, looking expectantly at Celes and Rino, but the two just tilted their heads in confusion.

"Hmm? You can't use magic?" asked Rino.

"I understand your question, but it's kind of like asking if you can teach humans how to breathe," said Celes.

Demons were different from humans in that they were born with magical powers and the capacity to use them. They might be able to help with incantations, but they had no idea how to teach someone incapable of it.

"Right… But I feel like I can use it now for some reason."

Shinichi's body felt different from before he underwent his super-high-speed strength training. It felt like something more than blood was now running through him—something hot. At first, he thought it was the aftereffects of *Pain Block* or *Self-Healing Power Boost*, but that wasn't the case.

"I am not sure I completely understand. But if you feel that you can, maybe you should test it?" suggested Celes doubtfully after hearing Shinichi's explanation of this unfamiliar sensation in his body.

"All right! Let's try it, then. How do I cast magic?" asked Shinichi.

"It's easy. You just think *Become like this*, and say the name!" said Rino.

"Uh, that's it?" Shinichi, not entirely trusting Rino's explanation, looked to Celes, who nodded in agreement.

"Yes, I am not sure what you expected, but magic is very simple. My teacher told me, 'At its source, magic has only one possible effect,'" explained Celes.

"And what is that?" Shinichi asked.

"My teacher said magic is 'a way to alter reality to match your imagination.' Whether it's throwing a ball of fire or making a pillar of ice, it all comes from the same foundation, albeit with different results," elaborated Celes.

"So what about incantations and magic circles?"

"They are simply tools to help strengthen the image of what you want. You are much more likely to see the fire in your mind if you say *Burst forth, red flames* than if you tried to do it without saying anything."

Shinichi began unconsciously tapping as his understanding grew. He already had a conception of how words had power even in twenty-first-century Japan, as seen in the concept of *kotodama*, power words that manifest your desires. Outside supernatural phenomena, there was a scientific explanation for the effect of speaking things into existence. Professional athletes often engage in positive visualization exercises, thinking *I am strong* and *I can win* as a part of their psychological training, which helped improve focus and motivation.

"You should first start small. Try to imagine a flame," suggested Celes.

"Okay... Fire. Red, hot, blazing..." Shinichi followed Celes's advice, holding up the palm of his hand as he closed his eyes and envisioned a flame.

With breathless intensity, he imagined a flame about the size of a matchstick hovering over his palm. As he did, the strange heat in his body started concentrating in his palm.

"You can say whatever you like. Just believe that the flame you imagined will appear, have no doubt, and shout to release your power," continued Celes.

"Flame...burn, burn. *Fire!* Argh—!"

Shinichi snapped his eyes open, calling the magic word in English. When he did, the heat contracted and burst into a red flame burning above his hand.

"Whoa! It really appeared!"

"Shinichi, you did it!" Rino shouted happily, as if it were her own accomplishment, flinging herself onto Shinichi, who was still standing in shock. He wouldn't dare say that it was the softness of her prepubescent chest that broke his concentration, but the flame above his palm flickered out of existence.

"It went out. It's pretty hard to maintain," observed Shinichi.

"Of course. Magic can only be improved by practicing your ability to quickly, accurately lock onto an image and maintain it. This can only be improved with persistent practice." Celes's expression was serious, as if to say there was no way to cheat your way out, like with his high-speed strength training.

"I guess so. Well, they do say there are no shortcuts to learning," said Shinichi.

Even with strength training, he could improve the strength and speed of his corporeal body, but he hadn't developed the necessary skills to put his body to good use. A skilled warrior could easily handle a kid with a bit of physical strength. In the same way, even if he obtained the power required to use magic, he had to spend the time learning the skills to use it well.

"But looking at it the other way, that means there should be a superfast way to increase my magical power." Shinichi's face yet again twisted evilly as he thought of something new.

"Shinichi, you're smiling deviously again...," said Rino, who was a little scared.

"What kind of evasive trick have you thought of this time?" asked Celes, who was too fed up with him to even complain.

"Originally," said Shinichi, explaining his idea, "I had absolutely no capacity for fantastical powers, such as magic. That I can say for sure. However, when I did the strength training, it somehow became a part of my body. Why do you think that was?"

"Hmm, maybe when you trained your body, you also trained your magical powers?" Rino speculated.

"That is probably true for the King, but I'm a completely different case," said Shinichi, leaving only one answer. "It's because I had magic cast on me so many times! …I think."

"You seem just a little unsure about that." Celes stared at him coldly, which was not unexpected since he had no evidence to back up his idea.

"Which is why we'll do some tests to verify this theory. I'm asking you two, Rino and Celes, to cast magic spells on me! It doesn't matter what they are!" Shinichi didn't hesitate to surrender his body to human experimentation since he knew he could be resurrected even if he died.

Rino and Celes were a bit confused but did as Shinichi asked and began casting magic.

"Okay, here I go: *Physical Enchantment!*" said Rino.

"Good, good! Keep them coming!" encouraged Shinichi.

"Well then, *Harsh Pain*—," began Celes.

"Don't start off with killing me with your magic!" Shinichi cut her off.

"You will not die. It will just make you feel more pain than death," replied Celes.

"That's even worse!" He swore the maid would try to use every chance she got to test out uncommon magic so incredibly cruel that it would make anyone hesitate to cast.

Shinichi continued soaking up the magic spells until the two had completely exhausted their magical powers. And the results—

"Burn to ash in red raging flame! *Flame Pillar!*" ordered Shinichi, thrusting his palm outward along with the improved, slightly edgier incantation.

When he did, a cylinder of fire erupted, a little under a foot tall and an inch in diameter.

"Yeah! ...Well, it's a bit flimsy, but I'm totally leveling up."

Within half a day of absorbing magic, Shinichi increased the size of his flame from a matchstick to a gas stove.

But the people who'd been helping him sank to the floor behind him in exhaustion.

"Huff, huff... That's good...," panted Rino, trying to congratulate him.

"What...do you plan to do...? You're leaving us...spent...," complained Celes, still taking jabs.

Now dripping with sweat and gasping to catch their breath, the two of them had continued casting spells on him to the brink of collapse.

"Oops, sorry. Uh, thanks for going along with my plan," said Shinichi, running to the kitchen to fetch some water. "I'm not sure if this was very effective, though...," he muttered to himself.

His magical capacity wasn't increasing fast enough, even though Rino and Celes had exhausted their own magical powers on him. Both of them were acknowledged as top-class magic users within the demon world, but their combined efforts still weren't enough to help him out. If this had been a multiplayer online role-playing game, it'd be like spending half a day attempting to level up with the help of some high-level players and gaining one measly level.

"Well, there's no such thing as a free lunch," sighed Shinichi. The fact he was able to use magic was a small victory, even if it wasn't much. He returned to Rino and Celes with a water pitcher and purple fruits he'd grabbed from the kitchen.

"Ahh, water from the human world really is so delicious!" said Rino, joyfully finishing a glass of cool, clear water.

"On the other hand..." With a clouded expression, Celes regarded the untouched fruit.

"I know. It's hard and sour," said Shinichi, taking a bite of his share, which was just as vile as he'd expected.

The fruit looked like an apple but tasted worse than a bite of bitter butterbur.

"It'd be nice if there were some wild strawberries in the forest or grapes in the mountains...," fantasized Shinichi.

But the area around the King's castle was an abandoned and infertile valley—no edible plants in sight or wild animals that grazed their land. This meant they mostly ate those vile dishes from the demon world.

"The heroes aren't going to attack us for the time being, and it seems like we've started farming again. If we start raising some livestock now, we could probably start eating good food in about six months," Shinichi forecast optimistically.

"Six months..." Rino glumly realized it was further from reach than she'd thought.

"Well, we also have a ton of gold, so we could try buying food from nearby villages, and the surveyors might have missed fertile lands in the mountains—hmm?" Shinichi paused.

"Shinichi, what is it?" asked Rino.

"Do you have any spells that'll make food taste better?" He probably should have asked this question earlier.

He knew a lot of Japanese battle games didn't have these spells (mostly because it'd be too much trouble for the developers to include them), but some Western tabletop role-playing games did, especially those with traveling or rationing food as part of gameplay. It wouldn't be a stretch to assume they'd have a spell to conjure a feast in this fantastical world, kind of like a certain cat-shaped robot and its tools.

The two demons looked back at him with incredibly sour expressions.

"I tried once to see if I could, but..." Rino's voice tapered off.

"For starters, we can't properly visualize good food." Celes finished her mistress's thought.

"Ugh..."

Shinichi rubbed the corners of his eyes, pitying the two girls who eyed him with blank stares.

It made sense. By nature, magic was a way to alter reality to match your imagination. If you'd never experienced something, it'd be hard to imagine or manifest it.

"But, Rino, you've eaten bread before, right? And, Celes, you ate at that tavern. And everyone else had the butterbur and meat at the banquet." Shinichi sounded desperate.

Celes and Rino exchanged glances as Shinichi asked if these new experiences changed anything.

"The food was so delicious we couldn't fully understand it, so we can't re-create it," they said together.

"Ugh..." Shinichi rubbed his eyes again at this sad sight.

It might be impossible for Rino and Celes...but could I do it?

As a light bulb went off in his head, Shinichi regained his composure. He'd had ample opportunity to refine his palate in twenty-first-century Japan, known for its delicate and delectable cuisine. He also had enough knowledge of science and chemistry to understand flavor at its most basic level.

Delicious food... No, that's way too vague. I need something simpler. I'll go with "sweet."

"Shinichi?" Rino had grown concerned because he'd suddenly gone quiet, so she waved her hand in front of his face. Shinichi was so lost in thought he didn't even notice.

Sweet... Sugar... What's sugar made of? Well, its chemical makeup is $C_{12}H_{22}0_{11}$. Carbon, hydrogen, and oxygen... Okay, these are the elements this fruit needs.

Shinichi stared at his half-eaten purple apple (not its real name), formed the image in his mind, and gathered all the magical power in his body.

Become sweet, like sugar, sweet. Change into something delicious.

This mental image overlapped with reality. He chanted this spell to change its composition: "Smallest particles of matter, form new bonds, change your shape! *Element Conversion!*"

The spell came naturally, as he focused to release all the magic in him. A bright light surrounded the purple apple and then gently dissipated into thin air.

"Um, what did you do?" asked Rino, tilting her head in confusion at the purple apple in his palm. It looked exactly the same as before.

But the only way to know if it was a failure was to taste it.

"If it all goes to plan... Mm?!" Shinichi, bracing himself, took a bite. His eyes opened wide, and he shouted in surprise, "It's sweet! Too sweet! What is this, a lump of sugar?!"

It was as sweet as if he'd condensed red bean soup a hundred times over. In fact, it was so sweet it almost punctured Shinichi's brain, forcing him to spit out the purple apple.

"Do you require the *Antidote* spell?" Celes inquired.

"No, I think it's fine. The magic itself was a success. Just didn't get the proportions right, I guess," replied Shinichi, trying to calm Celes and handing her the purple apple. "Take a bite, and you'll see it was a success."

"Oh, look at you! Getting all excited by making a woman eat something covered with your saliva. You pervert!"

"You know you could just cut off a piece I didn't touch and eat that."

Celes bit down on the apple close to Shinichi's teeth marks, despite her previous remarks. Her eyes snapped open wide when a burst of unfamiliar flavor hit her, and she melted into a relaxed smile.

"It's so good..."

"Huh?! No, it's so sweet it burns!" Shinichi shot back, but Celes couldn't hear him. Instead, she smiled rapturously, just as she had at the tavern, and took another aggressive bite of the purple apple.

"Oh, it's divine. So this is what it's like to eat something sweet..."

"Celes, you're hogging it all! I wanna taste it, too!" cried Rino.

Rino couldn't contain herself any longer, biting voraciously into the remaining half of the apple.

"Mm, it's so yummy! Shinichi, did you always get to eat food like this back home?!"

"Um, ah, yeah, something like that," he stammered, unable to do anything but gently nod in agreement with Rino, whose eyes sparkled with joy.

What the—? Do the demons share the same flavor profile as the Americans? Do they have bad taste?

These creatures had different palates, far from those of the Japanese, who enjoyed more subtle flavors.

The sickly sweet apple completely vanished by the time Shinichi completed his thought.

"Oh no, there's no more left...," Rino observed sadly.

"Not to worry, Lady Rino. There are mountains of *gazak* fruit in the kitchen," said Celes, who rushed off like a gust of wind. She returned

with a basket of purple apples (scientific name: *gazak* fruit) and placed them in front of Shinichi.

"Now, if you would be so kind," she said.

"Uh, hold on just a second. I'm really tired from the spell...," Shinichi protested. He almost gave in to Celes's demand but held his ground.

After all, he was only a beginner, running out of steam after casting one spell. On top of that, it was difficult to rearrange the atoms in something so vile. His whole body shook with chills, and a cold sweat ran down his forehead and back.

"I see. That's quite unfortunate," said Celes.

"Shinichi, are you okay?" asked Rino.

The two girls finally noticed his critical condition and used handkerchiefs to dab away his sweat. They went to boil some water to warm him up. But—

"It's unfortunate Lord Shinichi can't cast recurrent spells... But that means if we increase his magical powers, it'll be possible to raise his production of sweet apples," Celes calculated.

"Good call! Okay! Shinichi, let's keep our spirits high and resume our training!" Rino insisted.

"...Huh?"

"*Physical Enchantment!* And again, *Physical Enchantment!*"

"*Toughness! Insomnia! Resurrection! Reservation!*" shouted Celes.

"Wait, how much more do you plan to make me work?!" Shinichi wailed.

A company with unpaid overtime paled in comparison to their demands. He desperately tried to stop the two girls but couldn't derail them, especially now that they knew this new flavor.

After five days of training literally to death, Shinichi rapidly graduated from a beginner to an intermediate magic user. Despite this, he was still unable to magically change the atomic composition of the apples in rapid succession. But he had created something that hadn't existed in this world with the help of twenty-first-century knowledge and, of course, by cheating.

All this meant they were prepared to take on the new hero.

The Goddess's hero Arian woke up early.

The sky was just starting to get brighter. Before any of the other guests were awake, she was already out of bed and dressed for the day.

"Good. Up at a decent hour today," she said, tying her scarf around her neck.

She'd accidentally overslept a few days ago, but she wasn't going to repeat the same mistake. After smoothing out her bedsheets, she went down to the tavern on the first floor.

"Good morning!"

"Ah, lively as usual I see," remarked the owner as he wiped down a table. With a single fluid movement, Arian grabbed a mop and started cleaning the floor. "Miss, you're a customer. You know you don't need to help, right?"

"Yes, but I'm a hero!"

"That doesn't really answer my question."

The two shared their usual morning exchange as they polished the inside of the tavern.

"Here. A token of my thanks," said the owner.

"Ah, thank you very much!" said Arian with a small cry of joy as the proprietor gave her some dark bread, and she began to eat.

"Miss, I'm sure you make a good living. Why are you staying here at my little run-down inn when you could buy your own house?" asked the owner. Arian gave an awkward smile in response.

"I'm always out of town, fighting monsters. If I bought a house, it'd just get coated in dust."

"Ah, right. Well, what if you lived at the church? You're the Goddess's hero and all. I'm sure the priests would love it if you did."

"Oh no, I'm not very good at living with a lot of other people..."

"Ha-ha, so you're a bit shy even though you've got so much energy. If you continue like this, you do realize you'll be a loner for the rest of your life, right?"

"Urgh..."

The dark bread got stuck in Arian's throat when the owner poked a sore spot of hers.

"Sorry, sorry! This one's on me," he insisted, placing a mug of ale in front of her and going in the back to prepare some soup.

"Friends, huh...?" murmured Arian, alone at the counter, washing down the bread with a gulp of ale.

There were quite a few people who'd tried befriending her in the past, like Ruzal, the runaway knight. He'd kept trying to contact her after she beat him in a spar, but she never replied. She wasn't full of herself, and she didn't dislike him or anything. It's just—

"Okay, time to train," she said, slapping herself to chase away her dark thoughts before leaving the tavern with her sword in hand. She headed toward the massive castle walls surrounding the city.

"Good morning!" she greeted a familiar face at the gates.

"Ah, Miss Arian, I see you're hard at work again today," replied the guard.

She exchanged pleasantries with a guard with whom she was well-acquainted as she slipped through the gate. Outside the walls, the expansive land and its fertile soil were divided into large plots for farming. But the three-hundred-yard circumference around the city walls was empty, used for warfare. This is where Arian practiced.

"Kya! Hah!"

Her red, shoulder-length hair stuck to her cheeks with sweat, but she paid no mind and continued swinging her sword. Her attacks were faster than the eye could see. She stopped her sword near her midriff, and the aftereffects from her movements gouged the earth with air pressure. Her deadly sword could easily cleave a knight wearing full plate in two.

As she quickly swung her sword, her face remained grim.

"...This won't work. This just isn't enough to win," she said weakly, stopping after just ten thousand swings.

Though these strikes could split steel, she couldn't manage to put a single scratch on the Blue Demon King, causing her to retreat. She knew she wouldn't be a match for him even if she trained for years.

"But what should I do...?"

Even though she couldn't see it herself, there was no denying that Arian was a sword-fighting genius. She always fought alone and always won, which was why she was in a slump. The Demon King towered over her like a massive wall, and she couldn't find a way over it. He was the first obstacle she'd ever encountered, and she had neither a master swordsman to teach her nor companions for support.

"No, stop. I just need to keep trying!"

She had a tendency to spiral into dark, lonely places when alone, but she energetically threw herself back into her practice. She continued until the sun reached its highest point before thinking about taking a break.

"Arian, I see you're working hard again today," a familiar, gentle voice called out from behind her.

"Bishop Hube?! Why are you so far from town?" Arian was shocked to see the serene face of Bishop Hube, the highest authority of the church in the Boar Kingdom.

"It was on the way. I just finished attending the morning audiences and was about to go back to the church," he said.

It was true that his duties by the king's side were during the morning and he worked in the church afterward. However, the church was right next to the castle, so there was absolutely no need for him to come out of the city walls.

"I appreciate your thoughtfulness," she said with a beaming smile. It didn't reveal that she'd noticed the lie.

"How's your practicing going?" he asked. His smile had no underlying motives.

"Well..."

"From what I saw, it seems that it'll take some time before you can challenge the Demon King again."

"...I'm sorry," apologized Arian, bowing her head deeply.

"Worry not," replied Hube, gently patting her on the shoulder. "If you cannot defeat him, no one can."

"But that..."

"Have faith in yourself, Arian. I selected you, and you are the strongest hero." Hube's words had an impact on Arian, who wore an expression of confusion mixed with humility.

Arian had made a living hunting monsters—animal mutants that absorbed large amounts of magic—up until a year ago. Traveling from place to place, she eventually came to Boar Kingdom. That's when she met Bishop Hube, who convinced her to accept the Goddess's blessing and become a magnificent hero.

"Since becoming a hunter, you've been undefeated, right?"

One could say the hunters killed monsters that attacked people, with the safety of their communities in mind. It would be more accurate, though, to say many hunters were criminals, and good, honest folk often talked about them behind their backs. This was true for Arian: She was a young maiden who had single-handedly slaughtered many monsters, though she was feared at the same time for her abnormal strength.

However, that all changed completely when she became a hero.

"You've been granted the protection of our Divine Goddess. You cannot die anymore. You've become a holy warrior who knows no enemies."

She had the stamp of approval from the great defender of all humanity, Elazonia, the Goddess of Light, worshipped by all. Becoming a hero was proof of one's character. Thanks to this, Arian went from a person who was feared to one revered by many.

And yet—

"Bishop, mine is far from the grand existence of the great holy warrior you speak of," said Arian, rejecting his high praise as she gripped the red scarf around her neck.

Hube saw Arian's fear and took his hand from her shoulder.

"I apologize. I have no intention of placing such a burden on you."

"Please! You don't need to apologize! You're the entire reason I was able to become a hero..." Arian shook her head and looked down, flustered and unable to find the right words.

Hube gently smiled again at the befuddled figure in front of him.

"I know. Anyway, maybe we should grab something to eat together and—"

"Ah, here you are," came a voice, unexpectedly interrupting the bishop's invitation.

Hube looked up. Before him stood a boy with black hair and black eyes, wearing leather armor with a sword at his waist. Behind him stood a beautiful silver-haired woman. For some reason, she was wearing a maid outfit, and he could feel strong magical powers emanating off her.

Hube had a strange feeling of déjà vu.

Before he could remember the source, the boy stepped in front of Arian, ignoring Hube.

"It's nice to meet you. My name's Shinichi," he said.

"I am Celestia, but please call me Celes," added the maid.

Arian politely responded to the friendly introductions.

"Hi, my name's Arian," she said.

"And is there anything that we can do for you?" inquired Hube, hiding his irritation behind a smile.

The boy didn't bother to look at the bishop, instead extending his right hand toward Arian.

"I feel blessed to meet the world's strongest hero," he said.

"I'm really not that special… Um, what's with the hand?" asked Arian.

"Oh, sorry. It's a custom where I come from—called a handshake. It's a friendly greeting, you know. Two people grip each other's hands," the boy explained.

"Okay, let's handshake, then!" exclaimed Arian, unable to refuse his request and gripping his hand.

"…Such slender and beautiful hands," he observed.

"Huh?! N-n-no, they're not! All I do is swing around a sword, so they're dirty and covered in calluses!" Turning bright red, Arian contradicted the unexpected compliment, but the boy just smiled gently and stroked her hand.

"No, they're beautiful. You have gentle hands that show all the effort you've put into saving people."

"S-s-stop, don't make fun of me!" Arian withdrew her hand, but her face turned a deeper shade of red, and her whole body quivered with joy, like a dog wagging its tail.

Hube's smile stiffened slightly as he watched their exchange.

"And what is it we can do for you?" he asked a second time.

"Arian, I've been looking for you to ask something," said the boy, finally answering the question but ignoring Hube as he looked deeply into Arian's eyes. "Let me help you defeat the Demon King."

"Huh?"

"Actually, no. What I'm trying to say is…join me, and I'll let you defeat the Demon King," he said. His corrected statement oozed hubris.

"Whaat—?!" Arian shrieked in surprise.

Prior to this, everyone she'd encountered was humble and had treated her as their superior, as expected. She was obviously so much stronger than any of them. And yet, this boy made no attempt to flatter her. In fact, he delivered this request as if he were her superior.

"Are you serious?" asked Arian. Her heart was beating not out of discomfort but shock that someone had addressed her in such a manner.

Humble by nature, Arian wasn't overly prideful about her strength, but she did have confidence in her abilities and a good eye for evaluating her opponent's potential.

"I don't mean to be rude, but I don't think I can beat the Demon King working with someone weaker than me," she said.

"I agree. I applaud your desire to fight the demons, but there's nothing to be gained from recklessness," added Hube, chuckling as he looked at the boy from head to toe. "You aren't a hero of the Goddess, are you?"

"So what?" replied the boy.

"Ha-ha, it seems there's no point in talking, then," scoffed Hube.

Hube wasn't wrong.

There was a huge difference in fighting style between a hero who'd always come back to life and a normal person who'd die. A hero was victorious upon defeating their enemy, even if they themselves died or their body was completely destroyed. After all, they were immortal. The Goddess's divine powers could teleport and reconstruct their corporeal form from scratch. This allowed a hero to fight in lava or nonchalantly use self-destructive magic.

However, this was not the case for a normal person.

Before anything else, victory for a normal person meant getting home alive. In the worst-case scenario, they'd die if they didn't have companions who could bring their corpse back to civilization, even if their body was intact.

All of this led to a fundamental difference in mental preparedness—a fatal difference in battle. It was for this reason that the knight's party consisted of all heroes while Arian continued to fight alone.

Although that wasn't the main reason she was a lone hero...

"You'll never receive the Goddess's protection with your haughty attitude. Don't throw your life away. Go home," said Hube. It was just a politer version of *Get out of here, small fry.*

The boy didn't seem to mind, instead smirking slyly and making a suggestion.

"Well, at least let me prove myself in a match. If I score even one point, we work together. If I lose, you can grill me, bake me, do whatever you like with me."

"Uh, well..." Arian hesitated.

"Are you not confident you'll win?"

"Hmph." She might have been a hero, but even Arian got riled up if someone mocked her or implied she lacked courage. "Fine! If I lose, I'll be your companion or whatever!"

"All right. 'Whatever,' you say?" he asked deviously.

"Leading her around the town in nothing but a collar and a leash is a level of depravity without precedent," said the maid, opening her mouth for the first time.

"That's not what I'm saying!" shouted the boy as he drew his sword from the scabbard at his waist. He turned back to Arian. "If my sword touches any part of you, I win. If you surrender, I win. Sound good to you?"

"Yep, that's fine," replied Arian as she slowly drew her sword, holding it to eye level. "I won't hold back just because we're sparring, though," she continued, the smile fading from her face as if the warmth was leeched away. "Don't get mad if I accidentally kill you."

She was not the bright and cheerful girl from before. She was humanity's strongest hero—a master of sword and magic.

Facing her was the daring young boy with a cold sweat on his brow.

"You wish," he said, smiling fearlessly, as if to say it'd be a good experience to die once. He kept his distance, though.

"One of a hero's duties is to put foolish children in their place. I'll handle the aftermath and clean up, so feel free to go all out," said Hube. In other words, *Kill him, and I'll resurrect him.*

Arian was surprised the bishop could give such a violent command with a smile on his face, but she didn't take her eyes off the boy.

"You can start whenever you want," she said, confidently giving him the first move.

He didn't hesitate to take her up on the offer.

"All right, I'll give you everything I've got."

The boy lifted his sword in one hand, holding it straight out at chest level. To make the most of this opportunity, he used his newfound magical powers to cast a fatal spell at Arian, who'd stopped blinking to watch his every move.

"My fiendish blade, my deepest secret—*Light!*"

He cast the most basic of basic spells.

But it was a serious hit against Arian, who'd been staring at him with her eyes wide open.

"My eyes, my eyes—!"

"Such a cowardly ploy!" shouted Hube angrily, seeing Arian bent over.

That wasn't the end of his dirty tricks.

Arian was trying to use her sense of sound, instead of sight, to discern her opponent's location, when she heard something rolling up to her.

Huh, a ball?

The moment she started to wonder why—

KABOOOOM—

The roar almost split her eardrums and pierced her body.

"Ah, gah—!"

Compared to this, the massive black wolf's howl seemed like a mosquito's quiet buzzing, and it did more than just destroy her ability to hear.

Everything's spinning...oh no...

The sound had been strong enough to destroy parts of her inner ear needed to control her balance. She'd never encountered anything like this while fighting monsters.

Unable to stand, she fell to her knees when a second ball-like object rolled toward her and exploded.

PSHHHH.

The moment she realized she was surrounded by some sort of smoke, she was overcome by a sneezing fit and an extreme urge to vomit.

"Gghah, gyah—!"

The delicate membranes in her throat, nose, eyes, and tongue stung, and her tears and mucus flowed uncontrollably. Four of her five senses—sight, smell, hearing, and taste—were obliterated, and the world's strongest hero was as helpless as a newborn babe.

The boy gently lifted his sword toward Arian, who was completely unable to sense anything around her.

"Full Healing."

The moment before the strike fell, all of Arian's senses were completely restored.

"Ah?!"

"Tch..." The boy clicked his tongue at Arian, who had only been stunned momentarily and was now advancing on him with her sword.

"Don't you think it's more cowardly for an onlooker to interfere in a match?" accused Shinichi, looking for the first time at the bishop who had interrupted their fight.

"The Goddess does not accept victories gained through underhanded tricks." Wearing a warm smile, Hube appeared to be almost gloating, but Arian scrunched her eyebrows together when he admitted to casting the healing spell.

"Bishop, he's right. Please don't interfere in a serious match."

"You're a hero chosen by the Goddess, and there's no need for you to give this cowardly boy a fair fight."

Arian narrowed her eyes as she looked at the bishop who was trying to evade her comment.

"Bishop, there's no such thing as cowardice or integrity in a fight. You fight to win," she said.

"......"

"Ha-ha-ha, it seems the hero knows what she's talking about. Our honorable bishop here just spends his time kicking his feet up at the church," jeered the boy with a malicious grin to the silent Hube. "Beautiful ideas like integrity and virtue have no place in a death match. The winner lives, the loser dies...though I'm surprised an undying hero would know anything about dying."

"I've been fighting since before I was a hero," said Arian.

"...I apologize." The boy offered a sincere apology.

And then he readied his sword again.

"Cowardice has no place in a fight, so I won't say you're disqualified for cheating. But I won't be so nice next time," Shinichi declared.

"Yeah, if it happens again, I lose," agreed Arian.

"......"

Hube's smile hardened even more, but the two faced off again, taking no notice.

"Just so you know, I won't fall for that again," said Arian. But once more, she let the boy make the first move, feeling incompetent for requiring the bishop's help.

"I know," he replied, his smile widening at the girl's stupid honesty as he reached into the pouch at his hip.

Is he going to make more noise or release smoke?

There was obviously no way Arian could know about grenades or tear gas, but she'd guessed he used some magic tools. She braced herself, observing the situation to avoid any impending danger. From his pouch, the boy drew something different from before. It was a glass vial.

"I predict you'll want to surrender when I open this." The boy struck a strange pose and pointed at Arian, but she didn't move a muscle.

Is it a bewitching or charming potion?

Arian's body was protected by massive amounts of magical power, giving her a strong resistance to magic spells. She didn't have immunity against physical phenomena—like his previous attacks with light, sounds, and smells—but she was confident she could deflect magic exerting psychological control, no matter how powerful it was.

As if he'd read her mind, the boy smiled as he put his hand on the lid of the vial.

"I'll explain. You might be able to endure pain, but you can't resist pleasure!" he declared, opening the vial and releasing its contents.

With the help of some magic, he'd created its contents, distilling it to its most potent scent—the smell of something delicious.

"It—it's sweet?!"

Despite the distance between them, Arian could immediately smell it, the sweetest of sweet fragrances. Its scent almost melted Arian, who'd never really eaten candy, from the inside out. This fragrance didn't exist anywhere else in this world.

The boy triumphantly showed off the liquid in the vial.

It went by the name vanilla essence.

"Hmm, it really does smell nice. Do you want to try some?" he asked.

"Yes!"

The boy paused a moment after Arian nodded without hesitation, then smiled wickedly.

"Then say you surrender."

"Ah, I..."

"What are you waiting for? If you lose, we'll just work together, and we can disband if you really hate it. You're the stronger one, so you can just throw me away whenever you want."

"Bu-but..."

Arian's stomach gave a cute gurgle as she tried very hard to resist. It was just about noon, and she'd done more than ten thousand practice swings. She was starving. It was difficult for her tired and malnourished body to resist this sweet and enticing aroma.

"Just say you surrender. Do that, and all this is yours."

"A-augh... No, I can't do that!" cried Arian, tearfully pushing away the evil temptation.

"Well, I guess we don't need this, then," said the boy, suddenly throwing the vial to the ground.

"Aaaaaaah—!"

The earth soaked up the sweet smell, the fiendishly entrancing liquid. Arian screamed and closed in on the boy.

"Wh-why would you do that?!"

"You said you didn't need it."

"That doesn't mean you have to throw it away!"

"I agree. Throwing away my Lord Vanilla Essence! Should I burn you to death?" threatened the maid.

"Celes, you, too?! I let you try some when I made it!" protested the boy, flustered that the maid was also angry and advancing on him, but he thrust his left hand into the pouch at his hip. "Hey, calm down. I have more."

"Oh, good...," said Arian, letting out a sigh of relief when she saw the vial.

The boy looked at the hero, no different from a normal girl, and smiled as he spoke.

"By the way, can I say something?"

"What?" she asked.

"One point. I win."

"...What?"

Grinning deviously, the boy held the vial in one hand and his sword in the other.

And his sword was definitely touching Arian's torso.

"Aah—!"

"How about that! Even a weakling can win with a little creativity," he said to the shocked Arian as he dropped his sword and offered his right hand. "With my intellect, I'll make sure you win. So shall we work together?"

He didn't ask to work under her or for her to work under him. Instead, he asked to work together. Not only had he proven himself, but he'd phrased his request in such a way that the loser, Arian, had only one possible response.

"Yes, let's work together." As she gripped the boy's hand, her face was a mixture of uncertainty and embarrassment.

"All right, have this as a symbol of our new alliance."

"Aah, thank you!"

Arian excitedly opened the lid of the long-awaited vial. She took in a deep breath to breathe in the sweet smell, her heart pounding in anticipation as she brought the vial to her lips and—

"—ngh?!"

"It's admirable you're honest, but you should be careful you aren't deceived. This lesson is the best present, isn't it?" asked the boy.

Overcome with a horrible bitterness and spiciness, far from the liquid's enticing scent, Arian shouted soundlessly at the boy who flashed her a crooked smirk.

From afar, Bishop Hube watched the two as they began bickering like old friends.

"……"

For better or for worse, no one could hear the grating sound of his teeth.

"Would you please explain your plan now?" asked Celes, emanating a cold, quiet pressure like that of a blizzard. She'd forced Shinichi to sit upright on the floor of the room they'd taken at the inn in the Boar Kingdom.

"Well, it's a plan to defeat the hero," he replied.

"You've already indicated that much. I would appreciate greater detail." Though her words were polite, Celes's expression was sharp. "I don't think you'll betray us at this point, but I can't help but be concerned when you say you're going to defeat our Demon King, even when it's a lie."

"Ah, right, well…"

Despite her history of harshness, Celes had helped him quite a bit, so Shinichi had assumed it would be fine if he didn't give her all the specifics. There were reasons for him not to reveal his full plan.

"So I've been thinking about the 'Become Friends with the Hero to Take Her Down from the Inside' strategy, but I haven't really refined it yet. I was saving that for after we team up," explained Shinichi.

"Your strategy is to just wing it?"

"No, it's not that. If I don't know her personality, I have no way of breaking her." Shinichi searched for the right words to explain to the skeptical Celes. "At this point, we have no way of understanding how the heroes are resurrected. So we can't just use physical force to fend them off, which means we're left with psychological attacks. Do you understand so far?"

"Yes, you demonstrated as much with the five heroes before."

"Right, but if I'm honest, that was sheer dumb luck. There's no guarantee the same strategy will work again."

They got one with her claustrophobia, one with his fear of insects, one with an embarrassing video, and the last two with the fear of seeing their party destroyed. He was able to crush the souls of five people and ensure they wouldn't attack the King's castle again, but Shinichi chalked it up to good fortune. Maybe those heroes were weak-minded.

"Are you saying the people who attacked the King were psychologically weak?" Celes squinted, feeling as though he was indirectly insulting her master by association.

Shinichi nodded without hesitation.

"They were. I'm sure they're fairly strong if you compare them to a normal person, but they'd never been in that type of situation before."

Drinking dirty water, eating rotten meat, pushing their bodies to keep going no matter what they were subjected to, killing their enemies, even if that meant ripping their throats out with their teeth: Those heroes had none of that spirit.

"I imagine they did at first but lost it at a certain point," said Shinichi.

"By 'a certain point,' do you mean when they became the Goddess's heroes?" asked Celes.

Shinichi nodded ever so slightly at Celes, who was quick to follow his train of thought.

"No matter where or how many times they die, they always come back to life in a safe place. They get to keep trying, no matter how many times it takes them to succeed… Even the sharpest blade will rust and dull if left to soak in lukewarm water."

If he was being honest, Shinichi was pretty envious when he heard about these heroes and their gamelike capacity to respawn.

"They say failure is the key to success. Humans learn from failure and grow, moving closer to success. In my world, if you die, that's it. There's nothing after that."

If you didn't fail, you couldn't succeed. But there was no way for people who have committed the greatest failure—death—to make use of their experiences. It was illogical. It was wrong.

"For example, if someone almost drowns in the ocean, they'd take steps to never drown again, whether it be by learning how to swim or never going near water again. They'd learn and grow in some way. But if you die, that's it… It's stupid. It's irresponsible to tell others, *Don't be afraid to fail, just go for it*, and all sorts of lip service. That— Whoops, sorry. I got off track."

"…No need to apologize."

Celes didn't push him further, seeing the normally very laid-back Shinichi showing some strong emotions. She saw the scars deep in his soul, wounds that couldn't be healed, even with the miracle of magic.

"Anyway, those five were cocky because they knew they'd be brought back to life. It was the reason they had cracks in their armor and why they caved to such small threats. But that doesn't guarantee there aren't heroes who can endure any amount of torture, right?"

If that kind of person did truly exist, the demons would have no way of hurting them. If the heroes continued to fight the Demon King, they'd slowly get stronger and defeat him one day.

Ironically, they'd be able to defeat the Demon King because of his immense magical strength.

"We proved with my body that it's possible to increase your magical power by absorbing spells," said Shinichi.

"That…," began Celes, but words failed her when she realized their fatal mistake.

It didn't seem like the five heroes had gotten significantly stronger in a short period of time. But that's how the King and Celes saw it, and their perceptions were skewed by their own magical capacities. In reality, their magical power might have been increasing ever so slightly. Thankfully, the King summoned Shinichi after ten days, but what would've happened if they continued fighting for a month? Or six months?

"A hero who has no fear of death, never yields to torture, will fight with every last breath… It sounds like something from a fairy tale. But there are people like that even on Earth: Rudel, Häyhä, Funasaka."

"Were they humans?"

"Some people say they were the devil, spirits, or demons, but they were human. Probably. Definitely…"

If you peeled back the layers of history, there were definitely people who seemed like they used real-life cheat codes. How terrifying.

But in this world, their civilization was similar to the Middle Ages—with a little bit of magic. If their population levels were also similar, there wouldn't be even a billion humans in this world. The smaller the total population, the lower the chance of some extraordinary person being born. And if you thought about the size of this world and the probability of someone prodigious on this continent hearing rumors about another country and coming all the way to the King's castle to attack…was just about as likely as taking a direct hit to the head with a meteorite.

"We've gotten off track again. It's fairly likely we'll encounter a hero with a reasonably strong will. In all honesty, Arian seems pretty strong."

"That's true."

The girl was a ball of high spirits with a strong sense of justice. Add that to the fact that she fought alone before becoming a hero. She wasn't too hubristic about her immortal body, and she'd proven she had guts and a good grasp on reality. If they did the same psychological torture to her that they'd used on the knight and his party, she'd likely just spring back up and grow.

"That kind of person won't give in to pain or fear. So what can you do? The answer is appeal to her good nature and persuade her."

"…What?"

Celes tilted her head to the side in confusion as Shinichi smiled evilly, his expression far from the good nature he'd just been referencing.

"Just as I said. We convince her it's wrong and immoral to attack the demons and persuade her to stop."

"But we've been fighting against the humans expressly because talking is pointless and has failed in the past."

"Yes, it hasn't worked so far, and it failed with the king of Boar Kingdom. But that's why I'm getting close to Arian—to make sure it works this time."

"......"

Celes didn't ask any more questions. Her brain was close to imploding from confusion. Even though Celes and Rino were intelligent, they still didn't understand human customs. It must have been a difficult concept for people who hear *persuade* and think *fistfight*.

"Celes, do you know the most important thing needed to persuade someone?" asked Shinichi.

"...I have no idea," Celes replied.

"It's simple. The answer is that person needs to like you."

It wasn't the accuracy of your argument or the soundness of your explanation but having a good relationship with the other person so they'd always lend an ear, regardless of what you were asking.

"No matter how something is explained, humans think that their friends are right and their enemies are wrong. Who they like or dislike, who they're comfortable or uncomfortable with—they decide right and wrong based on their emotions."

Of course, there were some people who calmly and objectively looked at information to make a judgment call. Though Shinichi had only spoken with him briefly, the king of Boar Kingdom seemed like an intellectual. Perhaps out of lack of ambition, he'd lost his authority to the Goddess's bishop, who made all his decisions based on his faith.

"Kind of in the same way we explained to the king, we can explain to Arian: The demons have no desire to fight. They were just acting in self-defense. A peaceful resolution is still possible."

Arian was honest with a strong sense of justice. In addition to the tavern owner, many people had told him this. Her sense of equity was why she was trying to protect humanity by fighting against the demons. But what would she do if she learned the demons were actually good and the humans were at fault?

She'd likely apologize with her natural-born honesty and search for a way to end the conflict for justice's sake. But right now, she was wrapped up in her unwavering belief that the demons were all malevolent.

"I'm basically a stranger to her. Do you think she'd believe me if I went up to her and said, *Hey, the demons are actually good*? There's no way. But what would happen if we overcame hardships together and if our relationship became stronger? How about if we become close friends or even lovers?"

Is this fight truly right?

Are demons really that evil?

As they tell her this and she starts having doubts, they could push the idea with a little performance. For example, what would happen if Shinichi fell down a waterfall and Arian found him being cared for by a kind demon girl?

"Rino could work for that role. She's the daughter of the Demon King and a good girl."

The two honest girls would surely sympathize with each other.

"So their only hope, a hero they trusted and relied on, learns the truth and comes back to suggest a peaceful resolution with the demons. I wonder what the bishop would think when that happens, ha-ha-ha."

Bishop Hube was surely a strong magic user, but that's only if you were comparing him to other humans. He was no match for Celes or the King. As the bishop, he also specialized in healing and support spells, not so much attack spells.

Put simply, there was no way he'd be a match for the Demon King. He probably knew that, which was why he sent Arian to fight in his place.

Regardless of the final outcome, it'd be pretty interesting if she stopped fighting and forged a relationship with the devils.

"Will they make peace with the demons as requested by their hero? If that happens, the teachings of the Goddess would lose all credibility, and the number of followers would be driven to the ground." This was the best outcome: The fighting between the demons and humans would stop, and the annoying church would lose its strength.

"Or will they chase away the hero as a heretic, even though she's proven her abilities and become a public figure? If they do that, people might become more suspicious of the church, and more importantly, they'd lose their only strategy for defeating the demons." In this outcome, the church's strength would be seriously damaged, giving the demons an advantage in any future negotiations or battles.

"They'd be balancing on a tightrope. No matter which way they fall, they'll end up in hell. Ha-ha-ha, I can't wait."

"You're twisted," said Celes, taking her usual jab at him but nodding her head admiringly.

Arian was Boar Kingdom's—and Bishop Hube's—trump card. At the same time, she was their Achilles' heel.

"It's the same in a shogi game. The rook is so powerful, you're in a pretty bad position if you send it out and the enemy captures it. I just love seeing the expression on someone's face when they've got you in check and think they're about to win but you turn the tables, and they lose! Yes, nothing tastes better than that!"

"You're sick and twisted to the very bottom of your soul," said Celes resolutely, despite not understanding anything about his reference to shogi.

She realized something.

"So you'll be building a relationship with that Arian, right?" she asked.

"Yeah, I'll do anything for her to like me, and then I'll persuade her."

"In other words, you're talking about manipulating and brainwashing a pure and innocent young girl."

"......"

Shinichi didn't answer, averting his eyes.

"...Deceiving a virgin and making her your sex slave! Despicable."

"I've been leveled up from sick to despicable?! No, using sexual methods—"

"—is not what you meant. But you were thinking that it would be effective, right?"

"......"

Shinichi turned his face even farther away.

"You must let me eliminate you. For the threat you pose to all women, regardless of their race, species, creed…"

"You're not even going to ask for permission first? Wait, I won't do anything obscene—"

"Please wait a moment. I'll make you promise with a *Gaes* spell."

"You really trust me that little?!"

These were the two agents who'd successfully entered a relationship with a human hero, but their internal disputes would continue until daybreak.

Chapter 6

My Magazine Stash Has Worse

The day after becoming Arian's companion, Shinichi, Arian, and Celes grabbed a table in the tavern to discuss their plan of action.

"First, we need to get you a weapon," said Shinichi.

"Uh, a weapon?" Arian tilted her head in surprise as she sucked on a candy. Shinichi had given her some because he knew one of the most basic ways to someone's heart was through his or her stomach.

"Yeah, your weapon's too weak compared to your strength," he asserted.

"Really?" Arian pulled her blade from its sheath at her hip and stared at it.

Her two-handed sword was forged from iron and slightly shorter than a normal blade, for her to swing it in a dense forest, but thick so it could bear her strength. The instrument was sturdy but heavy with a poor cutting edge. In reality, it was closer to a thin club than a real sword.

"You've worked so hard to get strong, but your weapon's holding you back. So we have to get you something better."

"Hmm, now that you mention it...," considered Arian, aware of the importance of good weaponry from her experience fighting monsters.

Until now, she'd thought as long as it was strong enough not to break, any weapon was fine. After all, she was too strong to have experienced a critical fight and didn't really have an attachment to material things.

"You'd be so much stronger if you had a light, sharp sword," concluded Shinichi.

"But I'm not sure that'd actually make me 'stronger,'" replied Arian.

"This is why you're a moron!"

"What—?!"

Shinichi crossed his arms smugly and started lecturing Arian, who was confused by his sudden outburst.

"Strength is more than swinging your sword to build muscle or casting magic spells to increase your magical power. Strength is also about having the necessary skills to gather information and finding the right equipment."

"R-r-really?"

"For example, I heard you scratched the Demon King when you fought him."

"Uh-huh."

"What do you think would've happened if you'd used a magic sword that could cut through anything rather than this piece of junk?"

"Um..."

"Yeah, you might have won. Or at least, you would've given him a good fight."

There's the saying that only a poor craftsman blames his tools for his lack of ability, but it'd be more accurate to say a skilled craftsman knows how to choose the right tools.

"Say you give an unskilled fighter an excellent weapon: They wouldn't know the difference. But if we gave it to you, you'd be like a demon with a crowbar."

"Y-yeah!" Arian nodded, persuaded not by the two unfamiliar idioms but by Shinichi's assertiveness.

"So do you have enough money to buy a magic sword?"

"Money? Well, I have a little saved...," muttered Arian quietly as the owner of the tavern walked up with their food and overheard their conversation.

He responded with a short sigh.

"Son, do you have any idea how much a magic sword costs?" he asked sternly.

"Not at all," replied Shinichi.

"The cheapest you'll find is about a thousand gold pieces."

"Whaaa—?!" Arian let out a shriek. A soldier's yearly pay was fifteen gold coins. "E-even if I scrounged for every last coin of mine, I wouldn't even have fifty!" she said.

"That's not going to work, then," said Shinichi lightly as he did some mental math.

Would that convert to about a hundred million yen? Some katana go for a couple billion, so I guess that makes sense. I don't think we're being swindled or anything.

Then again, the value of works of art differed from that of items that served a practical use. His idea of pricing didn't apply to this world, so he couldn't make any generalizations.

"Anyway," continued the owner, "there aren't many folks who can make a magic sword anymore. The swords are so rare that, even if you had the money, no one'd want to give theirs up."

"Oh, really?" asked Shinichi.

"You mean to tell me you didn't know any of this and just casually suggested getting a magic sword?" inquired the owner, sighing again in exasperation.

Shinichi smiled and scratched his head as he sent a telepathic message to the maid next to him, eating her dark bread without a care for the world.

"Celes, are magic swords rare in the demon world, too?"

"No, not particularly. The dvergr make them every day," she responded.

"Ah, I see..."

"Do you know the hoe Kalbi uses? The dvergr made that, too."

"A magical hoe?! Oh man, I want one!" Shinichi insisted energetically. What the demon world lacked in food quality, they definitely made up for in technological advancements.

"But the King's fists are far stronger than their magical weapons. No matter how much effort the dvergr put in, their weapons all end up collecting dust in our shed."

"That's really sad..." Shinichi felt sympathetic toward the dvergr, though he hadn't met any of them yet. At the same time, he was fired up, admiring how training could lead to great strength.

Thanks to their conversation, he had an idea for the next part of their plan.

"What should we do? We don't have time to earn a thousand gold coins...," muttered Arian glumly.

"Don't worry, I've got a good idea!" Shinichi beamed with a sweet smile. He nudged her shoulder as he said, "I actually heard about a sword entombed in a cave."

"Ah, you did?!"

"Yeah, and I happened to overhear the location of the cave. It's watched over by a nefarious guardian, so no one dared go there and it has long since been forgotten."

"Wow, so the magic sword's still there!" Arian's eyes sparkling with excitement as she digested his story.

"Which means we'll need to prepare for a trip to get the magic sword."

"Yeah, just give me a second, and I'll get ready!" said Arian before dashing up to the second floor. Shinichi smiled and waved after her while the owner of the tavern watched and sighed for the third time that day.

"Son, when I first saw you, I thought you were a pathetic, scrawny boy. Just when I thought you'd beaten Miss Arian and joined forces with her, now you're going off on a wild adventure for a magic sword? You're a strange one," observed the owner.

"Strange is my middle name," replied Shinichi.

"Cut the BS. And finish what's on your plate." The innkeeper smacked Shinichi upside the head with his tray. Shinichi sheepishly started eating his cold soup.

"...Do you think he caught on to our lie?" asked Shinichi.

"I'm just worried an innocent girl is being fooled by a despicable man," said Celes.

"Well then, you have nothing to worry about— Hey!" Shinichi quietly added that last interjection to prevent the owner from overhearing their conversation.

"When exactly did you discover a cave with a magic sword?" asked Celes.

"Never. I'd like to know about it if there is one," replied Shinichi.

"...What?" Yet again, Celes found herself unable to follow his meaning. Her stone-cold expression lacked any emotion.

Shinichi replied with a familiar smirk.

"There is no cave. We're going to make one. In fact, we're going to make a heart-thumping, hair-raising dungeon and make Arian's opinion of me skyrocket to the ether."

"Uh-huh..."

Baffled by his explanation, Celes gave up trying to think about it further.

"The weather's so nice today! It's the perfect day for a trip!"

"Yeah, it's almost a bit *too* warm."

Together, the three of them left Boar Kingdom after buying preserved foods and other travel supplies and headed westward toward the mountains.

"You seem more upbeat than usual. Are you antsy to get that magic sword?" asked Shinichi.

"It's not that. It's just been a long time since I've gone on a trip with anyone, so I'm really excited," replied Arian.

"Ah..."

"Why are you looking at me with pity?! I know lots of people now!"

"The way you said 'now' and 'know people' really makes you sound like a loner..."

"Ugh..."

Arian began sulking, blinking back tears, as Shinichi patted her shoulder compassionately.

"*Why are you picking on her? Is it so you can make her your sex slave?*" asked a smug voice.

"*This isn't going to turn into smut!*" Shinichi shot back at Celes's telepathic query before comforting the hero.

"Well, now we're team members and friends, so you're not alone anymore," he said reassuringly.

"Y-yeah..." Arian turned red and looked down as Shinichi casually grabbed her hand. She squeezed his hand back as if to check his temperature.

"......"

"*Um, Celes? This is all for the King, you know. If you wouldn't mind, could you please stop glaring at me?*" asked Shinichi, unable to endure the icy cold stare. She sighed and changed the subject.

"*You mentioned we'd be making a cave that entombs a magic sword. Care to explain how and why you're doing this?*"

"*Ah, can you telepathically connect us to the King so I can explain?*"

"*With the King? One moment, please.*"

Unlike Shinichi, Celes only concentrated for ten seconds to get them on the same mental frequency with the King, dozens of miles away.

"*Celes, Shinichi, how are things going?*"

"*It's going. We're still in the middle of preparing to entice the hero to betray humankind.*" Shinichi explained his strategy to become close to Arian before persuading her to give up the fight against them.

"*As part of that strategy, we're heading to the western mountainside. I want you to use your magic to carve a cave and put a spare magic sword in there.*"

"*Hmm, I could do that much.*" The King explained he used to dig mountains into flat plains as part of his training. He nonchalantly spoke of his terrifying deeds like they were nothing particularly special before asking, "*Will that not just make the hero stronger, though?*"

"*The sword doesn't need to be so strong that it poses a threat to you. It just needs to be better than her iron one. I mean, the sword's just there to entice the hero and shift our power dynamic so it looks like we're relying on her. The real strategy lies in the 'trap' in the cave itself.*"

"*Ha, tell me more,*" laughed the King, knowing Shinichi had another morally questionable plan.

Shinichi's internal grin widened as he explained: "*I want Arian to be caught in a trap in a compromising situation. Then I'll come along and gallantly save her, and she'll be all like,* OMG, sleep with me. *Basically, she's bound to fall in love with me.*"

It was actually a phenomenon called "misattribution of arousal," where a person mistakes a heart racing from fear for the throbbing feeling of love.

"*Do you really believe it'll go that well?*" asked the King, incredulous.

"Well, it might be going a bit far to say she'll fall in love with me, but she's more likely to listen to someone who's saved her life, right?"

This would probably have an enormous effect on an honest person like Arian. As proof, Shinichi put his telepathic conference call on hold to strike up a conversation with the girl next to him.

"By the way, wasn't it that bishop who invited you to become a hero?"

"Yep. It's all thanks to Bishop Hube that I received the Goddess's blessing."

"Yeah?"

"Even after I became a hero, he's always checking up on me, treating me to dinner. He's really a great person. I've always thought this is what it might feel like to have your dad around, hee-hee."

"Oh, that's really nice of him."

"Yep! That's why I have to work extra hard to defeat the Demon King for the bishop's sake."

"Yeah."

Shinichi returned to his conversation with the King, while occasionally interjecting a half-hearted response to his exchange with Arian.

"As you just saw, Arian easily feels indebted to others. But she needs to feel more indebted to me than the bishop. Otherwise, any attempt to persuade her will fail."

"I understand that, but...," started Celes.

"If I'm not mistaken, it seems the bishop or whatever has hardly done much for her." The King finished Celes's thought. He was right: Bishop Hube hadn't really done anything of importance.

All the bishop did was invite her to receive her blessing. She was successful because of her own skill and personality. Also, he probably had an ulterior motive—getting control of a very powerful pawn. As for checking in on her at every opportunity and taking her out for food, well, it's obvious this middle-aged man had uncouth desires for a cute young girl. If he'd been in Japan, someone would have called the cops.

"This hero is...what you might call...simple. You know. Naive," offered Celes.

"Yeah, I agree...," said Shinichi.

As her enemy, he was grateful for Arian's naiveté, if not slightly concerned about her future.

"*Anyway, what type of trap do you have in mind?*" asked the King.

"*Well, I think it'd be more convenient if the two of us were alone...,*" started Shinichi. He hadn't forgotten his conversation with the hero, whose hand he was still holding, and said, "You know, I feel really safe when I'm with you."

"Oh, r-r-really?"

"I think you're the first person I've been able to let loose with."

"Yeah?"

"I'm so glad we've become teammates, no—friends."

"Hee-hee-hee, I'm glad we're friends, too!"

Arian didn't care about the respect, responsibility, or being relied on as a hero. As a loner, she wanted friendship: It was tantalizing like nectar, far sweeter than the candy Shinichi had given her and far harder to resist.

"...You're really sick," said Celes so quietly no one could hear.

Shinichi was too preoccupied with his conversation with the Demon King that he neither saw nor wondered what kind of expression she made as she said this.

"Ah, here it is. The cave that holds the magic sword."

After camping in the forest overnight, the three finally reached a large hole on the side of a mountain.

"Is this it? It seems kind of new...," said Arian, tilting her head to the side skeptically. The cave looked like it'd been forcefully hewn in the past day or two. There was virtually no moss on the bare rocks.

"I think it's all in your head. Anyway, let's go," suggested Shinichi.

"Yeah!" Arian forgot her concerns as her new friend pulled her forward, hand in hand. They stepped into the dark hole.

"Please watch your step," said Celes, following behind the two and casting a *Light* spell.

"You know, this is the first time I've ever explored a cave," exclaimed Arian.

"Really? Didn't you hunt monsters for a living? I thought you would've defeated monsters sleeping in caves and taken their loot or something," replied Shinichi.

"I'm not a burglar! I only fought monsters that came near civilization or threatened us. Besides, there aren't really that many of them."

She went on to explain that monsters are mutated animals that absorbed magical power, but they were still intellectually the same as normal animals. Consequently, they didn't exactly have great treasures or loot that humans might want.

"Yeah, but you're so strong! Don't you ever dream of defeating a dragon and getting superrich or something?" asked Shinichi.

According to Celes, dragons were as strong as—if not stronger than—the King. They weren't creatures that could be easily defeated, but it'd be a task worth trying for one of the Goddess's heroes. At least, that's what Shinichi thought. He didn't mean anything more than to use this as a conversation topic, but—

"...I suppose," said Arian vaguely, a shadow suddenly falling over her face.

"Huh? Did I say something offensive?" whispered Shinichi to Celes.

"Maybe she's scared of reptiles?" Celes offered without much conviction.

They looked at each other, not knowing what was wrong.

Arian put in a lot of effort to fake excitement to hide her true feelings and exclaimed, "Ah, I see something!"

Blocking their way forward was an uneven door carved from stone. On it, there was a message carved in colloquial terms, so that Arian could also understand.

—One man and one woman together may enter—

"What's this?" asked Arian.

The message was a trick to get the two of them alone together. Shinichi would only be able to put on his performance to save Arian if Celes wasn't there. But Arian didn't know that, of course.

"I don't really know. But it looks like only two people can enter. Celes, I'm sorry, but could you wait here?" asked Shinichi.

"As you wish." Celes delivered her line perfectly. They had practiced beforehand.

After this exchange, Shinichi took Arian's hand and placed a hand on the stone door.

"All right, let's go," he said.

"Y-yeah," answered Arian somewhat reluctantly. She almost said, *You know, this whole thing is kind of like a wedding ceremony*, but she turned bright red and kept her mouth shut as she placed her hand on the stone door.

When both of their palms were on the heavy stone partition, it swung open, and the moment they passed through the entryway, the door closed behind them without a sound.

"*How does this door work?*" asked Shinichi inside his head.

"*By using my magic, obviously.*" As the creator of the cave, the King replied to his question. "*I do not make magic tools, and the dvergr didn't have time to help me out, so I am using* Telekinesis."

"*So a manual automatic door*," joked Shinichi, pretending to move cautiously while remaining intrigued by this simultaneously high- and low-tech door. He moved on to his next question: "*So what exactly did you put in here anyway?*"

All Shinichi had asked the King to do was to put in something that would get Arian in a tough spot, so he didn't even know the details yet. But the King just laughed, refusing to answer.

"*Ha-ha-ha, I'm going to keep that a surprise until you see it.*"

"*Okay, I won't ask any further. But it's something I can defeat, right?*"

"*...Oh.*"

"*Wait, what do you mean by 'oh'?!*" Shinichi was suddenly very uneasy, but there was no time to modify the plan now. They had just arrived at their final destination.

"Look, I think that's it!" exclaimed Arian.

The narrow path in front of them led to an open space with a single sword in the middle of it all. The sword glittered in the same dazzling light as the holy Excalibur, which selected Arthur as king. Even from the distance, they could see it was a very fine sword.

"How amazing! The sword actually exists!" cried Arian excitedly, dashing out alone to the sword and hastily gripping its handle.

The moment she did, a black, semitranslucent goo fell from above and swallowed her whole.

"Ng...gah—!"

She was shaken by its sudden appearance, struggling frantically to escape the goop, but with every move she made, it wobbled in the opposite direction. It was keen on trapping her.

"A slime?!" shouted Shinichi.

"The worst type, called a gluttony slime. I had some trouble after getting trapped in one in my younger years," boomed the King in his mind.

"Is this really the time to have a chat?!" shouted Shinichi, accidentally responding to the King out loud. The black goo—the so-called gluttony slime—was beginning to dissolve its prey in front of him.

But for some reason, it started with her clothes.

"No way, slime play?! Nice! All right! Good job!"

"Ga, gabobbb—! (Don't look—!)"

He was watching one of his top three erotic fantasies play out right in front of him. Shinichi momentarily forgot where he was and what he was supposed to do. He even gave a thumbs-up.

But he didn't have another moment to spare. This might be a fantasy of his, but he definitely didn't want to watch her skin, muscles, and internal organs start disintegrating before his eyes. That would be the most terrifying way to die.

"Hang on, I'll save you!" yelled Shinichi, drawing his sword and slashing the goo with all his might. He was careful not to hit Arian, but it felt like he was cutting through water.

The slime didn't have much surface tension. For a moment, its body looked like it had been sliced open, but it quickly bounded back to its original shape. What's more, the tip of the sword started melting, as if it'd been soaked in acid.

"Shit, this thing is actually strong! What the hell?!"

Of course it was strong. The same gluttony slime had given the young Demon King a hard fight, because physical attacks were not

effective against its liquid body. The goo was quick to suck in its opponent. It reminded him of the shoggoth in the Cthulhu Mythos—the original slime—which was extremely unpredictable and dangerous.

"*How did you manage to defeat this thing?*" asked Shinichi telepathically.

"*I cast the* Self-Burning *spell while inside it, which burned it away.*"

"*Fire, of course. Oh, but the amount of fire I can conjure is...*"

Though Shinichi was an intermediate magic user thanks to his dirty tricks, it was doubtful he'd be able to burn away the massive slime, almost ten feet in diameter.

The only thing I can do to beat the slime in a way that doesn't hurt Arian...is this! Shinichi suddenly had an idea. Gathering his magic into his right hand and touching it to the side of his head, he conjured the image in his mind.

"*Search!*"

The brain often held on to residual information from distant, long-forgotten memories. Under normal circumstances, you wouldn't be able to find it in the sea of other memories, but his spell sought the information he needed.

"Augh... Got it," said Shinichi, laughing through the immense physical and psychological burden the spell put on his brain.

His greatest weapons were his twisted thoughts and the vast knowledge of a twenty-first-century Japanese citizen. They strengthened the image in his mind, and magic brought it to life.

Shinichi grabbed the pouch at his waist, pouring all his magical power into it.

"$(C_3H_3NaO_2)_n$, swallow it all, devour everything! *Element Conversion!*"

All the food and medicine in the pouch turned into transparent particles, which Shinichi threw at the slime. The pouch was unceremoniously sucked in by the big pile of goo.

But its liquid body quickly shrunk when the clear particles touched it.

"Ugh...gah, gah—!"

Arian was suddenly free, coughing up its transparent liquid as she watched it get smaller and smaller, eventually hardening into a clay-like consistency.

"*It's the material used in diapers—an absorbent polymer, capable of absorbing thousands of times more water than its own mass—not that you would understand,*" explained Shinichi smugly as he brought his sword down into the slime. It lost its softness, which had made it impervious to physical attacks, and was unable to withstand one strike from a partially melted blade. Its brittle body crumbled and moved no more.

"*Incredible—to think there was such a way to defeat it,*" applauded the King.

"*I never thought the day would come when I'd defeat a slime with diapers.*" Shinichi gave a wry smile in response to the King's praise as he looked at its remains. "*I didn't think it'd be this effective, though. Do magic-made objects have enhanced capabilities?*"

His magic-made fruit was sweeter than imaginable. The stun and tear gas grenades he'd used to defeat Arian, as well as the vanilla essence, were all more effective than their real-life counterparts, maybe due to Shinichi's imagination and magical power.

"*I hate to say this after all that, but magic's kind of scary...,*" he confided in his head.

"*You just aren't used to using it.*"

"*That'd be nice if it's... Ah, crap.*" Shinichi had gotten so caught up talking to the King that he'd forgotten to run up to Arian. He did so in a panic.

"Are you okay?!"

"Gah... Yeah, thanks, Shinichi. I owe you my life," she replied, looking up at him with a happy smile, even as she was seized by coughing fits and tears streamed from her eyes.

Shinichi grinned back.

"No, thank *you*."

"Huh? ...Ah," Arian said, noticing that Shinichi was very happy—looking at her body.

The perverted slime had dissolved most of her clothes and more than half of her underwear. She was almost completely naked.

"Aaaaaaaaaaaaah—!" Arian suddenly let out an earsplitting shriek as she tried to cover herself.

She curled into a ball and used both her hands to cover her body. She shielded him from looking at her…neck.

Hmm? What was that…?

She didn't try to cover her chest or groin, which brought attention to something else.

Shinichi had briefly seen an inexplicable *something* and used the *Search* spell to replay the image again in his mind. Afterward, he tilted his head to the side.

"Arian, um—"

"Don't look, don't looook—!" cried Arian, crying and screaming like a child at Shinichi's attempts to talk to her. She kept talking so he couldn't get a word in edgewise.

"This is bad. Let me—," he started.

"—die to atone for your sins?" came a sudden voice directly behind Shinichi, surprising him. Its tone was so cold their surroundings could freeze over.

"Ah! C-Celes?" asked Shinichi.

Behind him stood the maid who was supposed to wait by the stone door. Her normally expressionless face was replaced with a wonderful smile as she looked at the flustered Shinichi and naked Arian.

"You were taking a while, and I heard a scream. Naturally, I was concerned and came to check on you. But it seems I've interrupted your fun."

"No, I can explain! I haven't done a single inappropriate thing, right?" Shinichi desperately pleaded with Arian behind him and the King in his mind to help him escape the murderous maid.

"He saw. He saw, didn't he…?" whispered Arian repeatedly.

"Well, I must return home to read Rino a picture book."

The victim was only able to let out a whimper in a soft voice, and his witness cruelly abandoned him.

"Hey! W-wait a minute!" started Shinichi. He wanted to shout at the King: It was your idea to use the slime! But the maid mercilessly dug her nails into his shoulder.

"Do you have anything you'd like to say?" he asked sheepishly.

"...Just one thing, if it wouldn't be too much trouble," said Celes.

"Go ahead."

She looked at him expectantly with a cold smile.

Shinichi grabbed her by the shoulders as he proclaimed to her with a serious expression, "I really do prefer big boobs."

"I know, you sick bastard," she said, bringing her knee up to kick him directly in the balls. It wasn't hard enough to crush them but painful enough that he wasn't able to make a sound in response.

The boy wasn't so experienced or perverted that he'd think to thank his dominatrix.

Eventually, Shinichi was able to clear up Celes's misunderstandings, and the three of them took what remained of the magic sword back to Boar Kingdom.

"Ah, I'm seriously beat," said Shinichi after finally making it back to his room in the inn. He was more exhausted mentally than physically, and he threw himself onto the bed.

His mind wandered off to think about Arian, who seemed afraid to speak to him ever since the slime incident.

"I don't think she hates me, but..."

They'd hit some unexpected roadblocks, but his "*Ba-dum!* Arousal Misattribution Performance" strategy succeeded. In fact, the moment after he'd gotten Arian out of the slime, she'd shown gratitude and seemed fond of him. The problem was he'd seen her naked. It was normal to be embarrassed, but it was a bit strange she'd continue refusing to talk to him.

The reason she wore a dark, cold expression was—

Knock, knock.

"Shinichi, do you have a minute?"

Speak of the devil. Arian came by just as he thought about her, making him jump out of bed to open the door.

"Sure, come on in."

"Okay, thanks...," said Arian, hesitating a few moments before entering slowly. Her face showed resolve, as if she were a normal soldier facing off with the Demon King.

"There aren't any chairs, but make yourself comfortable on the bed," invited Shinichi.

"Okay..." Arian took a seat on the bed as directed. Shinichi sat next to her.

She was in a situation where he could basically push himself on top of her and she was completely defenseless, but she didn't have the mental capacity to notice.

"Um, Shinichi."

"Yeah?"

"You know, my... You saw it, didn't you?"

She couldn't bring herself to say what *it* was. She was clinging to the small hope he hadn't seen it, and she'd just reply with some joke about how he'd stared at her naked body.

Shinichi could see all her emotions. With this in mind, he decided to tell her in a straightforward way, instead of beating around the bush.

"I saw that thing at the base of your neck," he said, pointing at it, concealed by her red scarf.

Her face went pale, and she started shaking like a prisoner who'd just received a death sentence. Her expression was one of surrender as she undid her scarf.

Based on the whiteness and slenderness of her neck, one would've never been able to guess she was capable of injuring the Demon King. Right in the middle—near the location of a man's Adam's apple—there were fragments in neat pentagons with the crimson vibrancy of blood.

There were scales on her throat.

"I'm sorry I tricked you. This is my true form."

"Are those dragon scales?" asked Shinichi.

She nodded her head, on the verge of tears, apologizing.

"I'm a human with dragon blood. I was told I'm a half dragon," she said uncertainly.

She'd never met her father. Her earliest memories included being raised by her mom, traveling from town to town, and living life on the road.

"If someone was suspicious or found out about my scales, we

couldn't live there anymore. We were always traveling, but it took a toll on my mother, and three years ago..."

Her own mother had been adamantly against receiving treatment or requesting resurrection from the Goddess's church. They didn't have the money anyway, but there seemed to be a greater personal reason. Even now, Arian's heart ached because her mother refused to tell her why.

"I see," Shinichi said. Because he also understood how hard it was to lose someone, all he could do was nod.

"I took on the job of fighting monsters to support myself. My body's pretty strong because of the dragon blood," related Arian, cracking a weak smile. It went without saying this task was unsafe for a girl of twelve or thirteen at the time. "Everyone was happy when I defeated a monster. They'd thank me, the children would give me flowers, and the little old ladies would give me soup."

"You seem like the kind of person children and the elderly would like," said Shinichi. Arian smiled briefly again, but the expression on her face was quickly replaced with a dark look.

"There were just about as many people who were afraid of me."

It must have been hell for her hearing others ridicule her for being heartless. This was all because Arian could easily take down monsters a normal person didn't stand a chance against. What would happen to them if she turned her sword against them? Even a child could guess the outcome.

"That's why I wasn't able to live in one place for too long, and I just kept traveling."

She was in trouble if anyone found out about her true form, and her source of income disappeared once she defeated the monsters in the area.

"And then, about a year ago, I came to the Boar Kingdom, where the bishop approached me."

And asked if she wanted to become the Goddess's hero.

In the beginning, she refused immediately. She thought there was no way the Goddess would give her blessing to a half dragon, a mixed-breed monster. But—

"I thought if I became a hero, even someone like me could be accepted by everyone and live here..."

In fact, when she became a hero, the number of people who looked at her fearfully dramatically decreased. It went to show the absolute power of her new status and the blessing of the revered Goddess.

"But in the end, I'm still a monster. I'd forgotten that, gotten carried away when I became part of a team, when I made friends… I'm sorry," apologized Arian, bringing her head down remorsefully.

Her normal cheeriness was just empty bravado to cover her weaknesses. Her strong sense of justice was an expression of her adolescent desire to be accepted by someone—by anyone.

When Shinichi saw her true character, he thought—

"It's funny that you also have the custom of bowing your head when you apologize. What a strange coincidence."

—something as trivial as this.

"…What?" asked Arian, not really understanding what he'd just said.

Shinichi tilted his head in confusion.

"I get all that history leading up to you becoming a hero, but why do you sound like you're here to say your final good-bye?"

"Uh, like I said, I'm a half dragon and—"

"I don't understand," said Shinichi, cutting Arian off, as she frantically started to say the same thing again.

"Imagine being a hero with dragon's blood! That's super-duper cool!"

He spoke these words from the bottom of his heart, but for some reason, thc air in thc room went cold.

"…Are you being serious?" asked Arian, unable to believe what he just said. Her face was tinted with anger, not exasperation.

"Yeah, dead serious. A hero and a dragon, an existence that unites the powers of good and evil! Man, there's nothing more poetic than that!"

Yes, this was a classic trope, and yes, he might've been ridiculed for being a geek, but a classic transcended generations. What's cool was cool. You couldn't argue with that.

Arian couldn't stop herself from shouting at Shinichi.

"You're a liar! I have the scales of an evil dragon! I'm a beast, no different from the monsters or demons. I'm disgusting!"

"Oh, that's right," said Shinichi, finally remembering the conversation he'd had at the church upon seeing Arian grow increasingly stubborn and angry.

The priestess had said the dragons were evil creatures for killing the gods. They were feared and hated as much as the demons, if not more. It was likely a person with dragon blood would be seen in the same way. But this was one of the many instances where Shinichi's sensibilities didn't seem to match up with their worldview.

"See? You're thinking that it's disgusting, aren't you?" demanded Arian with tears in her eyes.

"Nope, not at all." Shinichi shook his head in response.

He looked at her neck again. He felt a bit like something was out of place, just because he wasn't used to seeing it. But he didn't feel a shred of disgust. He was born in Japan, the porn capital of the world, where snake women and spider women were viewed with sexual desire. It was insulting to imply he'd recoil in disgust from something as minuscule as a few scales.

"Yeah, I mean, they're definitely scales. But they don't have a gross sheen to them or anything. In all honesty, they're like little, twinkling jewels. They're sort of pretty."

"P-pretty?! Don't even joke about something like that!"

"I'm serious. I've only been telling the truth," said Shinichi.

Well, he was a con man, comfortable with casually lying to achieve his goals, but he wasn't so cruel as to lie to a girl about a genuine concern of hers. Besides, he wasn't a pickup artist and definitely didn't have the skills to manipulate women like that.

Even though that was all true, Arian stubbornly refused to believe him.

"If you really think that, then go ahead! Touch them!" said Arian, thinking she was calling his bluff and he'd find them too gross. But almost immediately, she was proven wrong.

"Uh, can I really?" asked Shinichi with obvious curiosity.

His face was colored with delight as he stretched his hand out to touch her neck, and he gently caressed the red scales, hard and smooth and a bit cooler than the skin around them.

"They're really different from the scales on a snake or fish, aren't they? They don't feel gross or slimy at all."

"Ah..."

"I wonder if they're made of keratinized skin like nails. Or maybe it's enamel like teeth. Or maybe similar to bone and made of calcium... Fascinating."

"Ngh...aahh!" Arian's cheeks flushed, and she let out a small, stifled shout.

Shinichi finally realized he'd gotten carried away by his curiosity and was running his fingers over her scales.

"Sorry. Did I hurt you?" he asked.

"N-no, I'm fine." Arian regained her composure when he took his hand away, but her eyes chased after his fingers longingly.

"Anyway, you believe me now, right?"

Shinichi really didn't care she was a half dragon. He hoped his actions had shown that, but Arian shook her head in discontent.

"No, you could probably just bear through all this...," she said.

"Then what should I do to prove it?"

"...Lick them."

"What?"

"...Lick my scales with your tongue."

She was basically telling him to kiss her neck.

"Are you serious?" asked Shinichi. His eyes opened wide in shock at her sudden request, but Arian seemed to have assumed the worst, as her face clouded over again.

"You can't do it. You really do think they're gross..."

"No, that's not it," said Shinichi, still confused.

"Then just lick them!" she begged. Tears started welling up in the corners of her eyes.

In some ways, this situation was almost too good to be true, but Shinichi's head wasn't filled with excitement. It was filled with confusion.

What the—? Do they have some mysterious custom of licking necks to prove themselves?

There wasn't any sort of custom.

In fact, she proposed it out of joy at having Shinichi touch her scales—the symbol of the detestable dragon's bloodline and the cause of her psychological torment. At the same time, she said it out of stubbornness and frustration toward Shinichi for treating her pain and trauma so lightly.

Oh, come on. Grow up… Shinichi sighed internally.

He weighed his own sense of shame against the various problems that might arise if he refused. He struggled with himself just a bit before drawing Arian's petite frame closer to his.

"Ah…"

"You're really much more difficult than I expected," he said before sucking on her neck like a bloodthirsty vampire.

"Ah, ahhh!"

Arian's body shook like she was hit by an electric shock the moment Shinichi's tongue ran over her hard scales. Shinichi thought there was no turning back now and forced himself to keep going, as his tongue danced across her neck.

Lap, lappa, shuupa.

"—gh!"

"…A bit salty," said Shinichi, removing his lips when Arian started to shake in larger convulsions.

"Ahh, ahh…"

As Arian looked at Shinichi with dewy eyes, her cheeks were flushed, and she breathed heavily. There was no trace of a little girl and her usual childish enthusiasm. In its place, there was the face of a passionate young woman.

"Shinichi…"

When she said his name, her voice was sweeter than the candy he'd conjured with magic. It scrambled his brains and smothered any semblance of rational thought.

"……"

Shinichi pushed her down onto the bed without a word, and she was silent as she closed her eyes. Their faces drew closer, and this time, his lips moved from her scales to—

Knock, knock.

"Lord Shinichi, do you have a moment?"

""Ah?!""

Just before their faces touched, they were interrupted by a visit from the maid.

"Wh-what should we do?!" cried Arian, hysterical.

"C-calm down, we weren't doing anything inappropriate… Ah no, yeah, we were," said Shinichi in a panic.

"Hello? You're making quite some noise. I'm just going to assume I may enter?" called Celes from outside the door.

The two jumped away from each other in a start, and the doorknob turned slowly as if to back them into a corner.

"Ah, uh…I'm sorry!" said Arian as she suddenly flung open the window. Before Shinichi could stop her, she jumped out.

"Wait! We're on the second floor!!"

"Soooorryyyyyy—!"

It seemed that his worries were for naught. The Goddess's hero stuck the landing perfectly and dashed off faster than a horse, as she let out a shout loud enough to wake up the entire neighborhood.

"You didn't have to run away like that…"

"Is that what they call 'the sensitive heart of a young maiden'?"

A hand reached out next to Shinichi to close the window. It belonged to Celes, who'd managed to enter the room at some point.

She went around to lock the door and chanted a *Silence* spell, a soundproofing countermeasure to coat the floor and walls, making the room entirely secure. It also meant no screams or cries for help would be heard outside the room, regardless of her torture methods.

"You do know what I'd like to say, right?" inquired Celes. Her gold eyes were harder and colder than steel, and her expression said that she knew all about his little love affair with Arian. She'd accept no lies or deception.

"You were watching with a *Clairvoyance* spell, weren't you…?"

"Of course. It's my duty to monitor and guard you."

It made sense, as there was a very small chance that Arian would've hurt Shinichi in order to keep her secret from getting out.

"But it's not part of my duty to be forced to watch you and that female copulate. This is sexual harassment."

"Wait a sec, we weren't going to copulate or anything—"

"Can you really, absolutely, certainly say it wasn't going to happen?"

"......"

Shinichi averted his eyes, saying nothing.

"Ahh... Did His Highness and Lady Rino really have to entrust themselves to this disgusting dog in heat...?"

"Now you're treating me like some animal?"

Knowing it'd be a waste of time, Celes swallowed her response that all men were wolves.

"Well, you could say I went a little overboard, and maybe I should've been more careful, but getting Arian to like me—," started Shinichi again.

"—is all for the plan, right? I'm well aware," said Celes, cutting off his excuses. "Which is why I am not angry about that. I don't care one bit if you're some perverted mongrel, licking some female's neck."

Her monotone voice was no different from normal, but she was strangely forceful in her response. Shinichi knew full well he was about to step on a land mine but said it anyway.

"Celes, are you......jealous?"

He expected her to spit out an insult about him being narcissistic and disgusting, while hitting him with an attack spell just weak enough to keep him alive.

But after a short moment of silence, Celes cast her eyes down and spoke in a way completely contrary to his predictions.

"...You said you liked me," she said sweetly.

"What?!"

"Oh, it's so easy to lead men on, right?"

"Stop screwing with me!"

Her prior timidness dissolved from her face, as Celes broke out into a wide grin. Shinichi cursed himself for being foolish enough to fall for her act.

"Okay, enough humor for now," said Celes, regaining her composure.

"Celes, I would've never guessed you liked comedy from your cool exterior. But you do, don't you?"

She didn't respond to his question, instead saying, "I have no issue with you making the hero fall for you. But are you sure you aren't falling for her?"

"Uh..."

Celes poked a sore spot, and Shinichi was unable to find the right words. He realized he might be the one caught in a trap he'd laid himself.

"To be honest, I didn't think Arian was this kind of person."

She was supposed to be a hero chosen by the Goddess, working hard to defeat the evil Demon King. At first glance, she seemed like some fairy-tale hero come to life.

"Loving justice, hating evil, honest, pure, strong—or put another way, a person unable to accept values other than her own—immature, stubborn, and violent. If that were the case, I wouldn't feel bad about destroying her."

But the real Arian was completely different. She'd lived her entire life detesting herself for being a half dragon. When she began fighting to feed herself, people thanked and accepted her—

She was just a pitiful girl who was only able to accept herself when she became a hero.

"She'd probably get angry at me and tell me not to pity her, but I can't help it. I found myself thinking that I would like to help her if I could."

"Because she is a cute girl, right?"

"Well, of course! That's the most important thing!" asserted Shinichi in response to Celes's joke.

Everyone knew he wasn't a saint. He was sick and twisted and accepted by the demons. He was the kind of person who had absolutely no urge to save humanity. But he was faithful to his narcissistic desire to help his favored few.

"Also, she reminds me of someone I used to know."

"……"

Celes didn't ask who that was. She saw a look in his eyes she'd never seen before. It held a certain loneliness, suggesting that person wasn't around anymore, not even on Earth.

"That's why I want to help Arian."

He didn't want her to suffer over something as trivial as being a half dragon. People might say he cared too much; he wouldn't hear them out. After all, he wasn't an ally of justice. He was an evil advisor employed by the Demon King. Getting rid of a girl's insecurities was just for his own satisfaction.

"You really are—," started Celes before clapping her hand over her mouth.

It'd be annoying if he saw the gentle smile on her face.

"Celes?" asked Shinichi suspiciously.

"I fully understand the situation," she said, returning to her normal steely expression. "However, you mustn't forget your original mission of subduing the enemy."

"No, I don't plan on losing sight of that," said Shinichi, nodding deeply to show her she didn't need to remind him. "We already have what we need if we're going to crush Arian."

They could tell the entire country she was a half dragon. Shinichi didn't care about her true form, and her close acquaintances, like the tavern owner, would likely be indifferent, too. But it wouldn't be this way with the vast majority of the population.

"They'll start treating her with prejudice, based on the Goddess's teachings and belief that the dragons are inherently immoral."

At the root of it all was a universal fear of those stronger than you, jealousy of those more successful than you, and revulsion of those different from you, like a half dragon. Also, when the person in question is a cute girl, these negative emotions manifested in the forms of misogyny from men and envy from other women.

"Seeing a person unhappy is like a drug. People love tearing others apart in the name of justice," continued Shinichi.

Unfortunately, prejudice and injustice were still rampant on twenty-first-century Earth. They'd likely still be there in the distant future, even as humans travel across the universe.

"I just don't understand. She's the strongest, which means she's right. Isn't that the only thing that matters?"

"I like that demon logic is so straightforward, but no," said Shinichi, smiling dryly at Celes racking her brain to understand. He continued speaking. "Anyway, it's possible to eliminate Arian by telling everyone she's a half dragon. She'd likely be upset, which also means it'd be easy to console her and become closer to her."

"But you wish to find another way?"

"Yeah," said Shinichi, nodding in response to Celes's question, then falling silent.

When he was ready to talk, he said, "I want to talk to the King."

"As you wish," replied Celes, sending a telepathic communication in the direction of her master's castle.

However, the voice Shinichi heard in his head was that of a cute girl.

"*Shinichi, what're you doing so late into the night?*" she asked.

"*Rino? Is the King out?*"

"*He's here next to me. He was just reading me a story.*"

"*Is something wrong, Shinichi?*" came the King's voice.

"No, nothing's wrong per se...," replied Shinichi hesitantly.

He was surprised he was connected to Rino, like an amateur radio enthusiast trying to find a signal. It made him worried they should put some magic in place to keep their conversations from being overheard.

But he didn't have time right now to be concerned with the smaller details.

"*I guess it's convenient. Listen closely, Rino.*"

It would be a mistake to go against her wishes. Rino and her desire to eat human-world cuisine were the catalyst for the King's actions, for summoning Shinichi, for this very moment. With this in mind, he told the King and Rino his own thoughts and feelings, leaving nothing out. He explained how unlikely it was that his plan would succeed, what would go wrong if it failed, and their backup plan.

The two were silent as they listened. The King was the first to speak, and his answer was simple: "*Shinichi, I entrusted this to you. Do as you see fit.*"

A king needed to accept the failures and successes of his inferiors, and he spoke confidently without wavering.

"*...You really are the Demon King,*" said Shinichi, smiling broadly and bowing his head in reverence, even though he knew the telepathy wouldn't transmit it.

Shinichi thought highly of the Demon King: He might be a muscle head, but his strength and generosity were unarguably that of a leader.

Following her father, his little daughter opened her mouth to speak as well.

"Shinichi, your strategy is too difficult for me to understand."

Rino was a rare intellectual in the demon world, but her appearance suggested she was only ten years old. It'd be cruel to expect her to understand the complexities of human society and Shinichi's sick plan to abuse it. But—

"I want to help Miss Arian, too. Being a loner is just so sad."

Upon listening to his story, Rino sympathized with a girl she'd never met and wanted to extend a helping hand.

"...Rino, you're seriously an angel," said Shinichi.

"Huh? What's an angel?"

"Oh, so there's a goddess in this world but no angels... Well, it means you're supercute."

"Whaaaaa—?!"

Through their telepathic communication, Shinichi couldn't see Rino turning bright red, but he smiled as he imagined it. And before her fawning father could get a word in edgewise, Shinichi hung up and regained his composure.

"Okay, now I have nothing holding me back," he said.

Now that he'd received the King and Rino's blessing, all that was left was to execute his plan. If it went really well, Arian wouldn't put up a fight about becoming an ally to the demons. Even if it were to fail miserably, the plan he put in place would still save the hero, even if he died.

No matter what, Shinichi was fulfilling his responsibilities to the King and Rino. He was going to trust in his own selfishness and place his money on a gamble with poor odds.

"I may be dealing the deck, but they're the ones picking the discarded cards. Well, what are you going to choose?"

Shinichi wasn't the one deciding the fate of Boar Kingdom and the demons. It was a hero with a secret to hide and the bishop with the kingdom wrapped around his pinkie.

Chapter 7

One Man's Bad Ending Is Another Man's Good Ending

Bishop Hube first met Arian a year earlier.

"What exactly is wrong with me?!"

"That's only for the Goddess to know. It's unfortunate, but I'm going to have to ask you to leave."

A priest took the young swordsman's arm and dragged him away from the statue of the Goddess. Watching after them was Bishop Hube, sighing and speaking quietly so no one could hear.

"Failure again."

Another failure to receive the blessing and become an undying hero.

That was the twentieth person who'd failed since he'd been assigned as bishop of Boar Kingdom two years ago.

"I guess it never goes as one hopes."

He thought things would be easier after Ruzal and his four companions became heroes, but things never went as one hoped.

"Not even I know your will," he said to the Goddess.

Though he was a bishop and a hero, he'd never heard the Goddess's voice and didn't know the requirements for becoming a hero. There was a stronger chance someone would become a hero if they excelled in martial and magical arts, deeply worshipped the Goddess, and had strong morals.

But even these rules weren't absolute. This was why so few people voluntarily sought out the Goddess's blessing, and many refused even if they were invited.

"Things will get complicated if we don't have more heroes."

Hube won the dangerous gamble to become a hero only after figuring out the odds were in his favor. This led to his appointment as the bishop of Boar Kingdom when he was in his thirties, which was abnormally young for someone in his position. It was all thanks to his talent and luck: He was undeniably blessed with natural-born ability, capable of mastering high-level spells like *Resurrection*, and the prior bishop passed away of natural causes at just the right time.

Hube had no intention of stopping now that he'd become bishop, though.

"I'm still looking for a hero who can enforce the Goddess's power in my place," he muttered.

There weren't many ways to achieve distinction within the Goddess's church. The main path was to improve your magic abilities, travel to remote villages, defeat evil monsters, heal the wounded, resurrect the dead, and spread the Goddess's message in order to bring more followers to the church. Hube had taken the time to do this and had achieved enough success to rise to his current rank. But he couldn't rely on his own skills to move up anymore.

He didn't have time to go gallivanting about on missionary duty. After all, he'd been given the responsibility of his own diocese. Not only did he need to heal numerous people every day, he was also busy making sure the king and lords of his country didn't act against the Goddess's will.

One of his only options was to bring in large amounts of money to the church through donations.

The other was discovering heroes and having them defeat monsters. The successes of heroes were also attributed to the bishop who found them. That's why all bishops, not just Hube, scrambled to gather the most excellent warriors and magic users and make them their own heroes.

"And Ruzal and the others are not very useful," Hube said in disgust.

Those five were strong if you compared them to your average soldier, but heroes needed to be far more…heroic. They needed to be powerful enough to destroy the legendary dragon that devoured the gods, the evil sealed deep within the earth. If they couldn't, they'd never be idolized enough to successfully spread the Goddess's will and make people believe in her.

"It'd take time, but it may be faster to mentor a child."

Though it was a secret from the masses, it was possible to train someone's magical power by absorbing spells. This method even worked for someone believed to not have these capabilities. But it only awakened latent magical powers, so not everyone could become a magic user or swordsman.

Not only that but this method required a lot of labor and time. For example, if a high-class magic user like Hube cast magic on someone until he collapsed for consecutive days, it'd take at least three months for one child to be able to use magic. But because he used his magic to heal and resurrect people all day, he didn't have enough capacity to use magic outside of work. It was questionable whether he'd be able to train one person a year. If all went well, though, that person would become a loyal pawn for Hube and the Goddess.

It'd be a gamble whether or not that person would be chosen as a hero or able to surpass Ruzal, but it was probably better than waiting around for something to fall in his lap.

It was around the time he really started considering that option when he heard the news.

"Bishop, there is something you should know about," said a single priest, appearing soundlessly behind Hube.

But Hube wasn't surprised. This priest was their shadow, a spy responsible for taking care of the darker business of the church.

"What is it?" asked Hube.

"A skilled monster hunter has come to town, known simply as Red."

"Red, huh?" Hube's brows knitted together slightly in disapproval at the nickname.

According to church dogma, the nefarious underground devils were partial to titles with colors in them like Black Demon King or Silver Demon Queen. Names with colors in them were not received well in the church. Though there were some arrogant fools who'd try to reclaim the title, spouting drivel like, *I'm the White Swordsman, even the demons should fear me!*

"And this person is a monster hunter?" asked Hube.

Though they made a living defeating dangerous monsters and protecting people, the Goddess's church didn't view them very kindly. Not because they were mercenaries, bandits, and other unsavory types who threatened people, but because they cut in on the heroes' and church's role of defeating monsters and protecting the peace, necessary to spread the Goddess's will.

That said, it's not like they could tell innocent folk to *Please kindly let the monsters eat you until the heroes arrive.* There weren't enough heroes to go around, so the church had to turn a blind eye to the monster hunters.

"Well, it's convenient if you consider it an opportunity to reduce the number of heathens," said Hube.

Knowing there was nothing to lose, Hube went to the location of the monster hunter, Arian. On an empty street on the fringes of the city, a girl stared wistfully at a happy family walking in the distance as her namesake red hair and scarf blew in the wind.

It was like an electrical current ran through him the moment he saw her profile. He knew she was the hero he'd been waiting for.

"Ms. Arian, right? May I have a moment of your time?" he'd asked her. His cool expression concealed his thundering heart.

Arian seemed a little surprised, but she quickly realized he was a member of the Goddess's clergy based on his clothing.

"Yes, what can I do for you?" she replied energetically and smiled, not a shred of her loneliness in sight.

Impressed by her strength, the bishop was now far more nervous to speak to her than when he'd received the Goddess's blessing.

"Will you become a hero of the Goddess, a guardian of the people?"

Arian hesitated at first, but he persuaded her by telling her she'd be respected by everyone and there would be nothing in this world she'd need to fear. After some resistance, she finally accepted his invitation.

And so she became a hero. In order to measure her skills, Hube had her fight in a match against her seniors, Ruzal and his four companions.

Despite her disadvantages, she was able to upset the match and secure victory. She'd shown as much promise as he'd hoped, and soon afterward, she was receiving missions directly from the Holy See.

Then the legends came to life, and the wicked demon army of the Blue Demon King appeared in Dog Valley. If she was victorious in her fight against them, Arian's name would go down in history, and the seat of archbishop, cardinal, and even pope would be within Hube's grasp.

Yes, their glory was so close at hand. However—

"Bishop, I apologize for bothering you after working so hard."

The priest's voice at his ear stopped him from dozing off.

"I'm very sorry, but we should get started soon."

Now fully awake, he remembered where he was and what he needed to do. He stood from his chair, and after passing through the church's antechamber, he faced the row of corpses at the end of the aisle. Once his morning duties at the castle were finished, it was his responsibility to tirelessly resurrect them one after another.

"Everyone, your hands, please."

He joined hands with a dozen members of the clergy, who'd been waiting for him, as they all formed a circle around one of the bodies.

"Our Mother, radiant in the heavens, our shining Goddess Elazonia, please hear our prayers."

The clergy followed Hube in unified prayer. At the same time, their magical power generated heat, which ran through their joined hands into the bishop's body. They could transfer and share their magical powers only because they all believed in the same Goddess under the same principles.

Their magic gathered as one, and Hube enacted the miracle.

"Kind and merciful Goddess, grant life to your child one more time. *Resurrection.*"

The magic power gathered in Hube's body and radiated out as angelic light, permeating the soldier's body. The hole in his chest closed in the next moment, and the revived heart began beating again. The dead soldier finally opened his eyes.

"Ah… Where am I?"

"You're in the Goddess's cathedral. Thank you for your service," said Hube, smiling gently at the confused soldier, who'd just woken up for the first time in a few weeks. The bishop then left him in the care of a priestess waiting behind him. He didn't have time to give a detailed explanation. There were just too many people to take care of.

Just when they'd resurrected six people, the cathedral was filled by the following exchange.

"Shinichi, I'm surprised you're so devout."

"Yeah, the massive boobs on the Goddess's statue really put me in the mood to worship."

"Oh, you! Don't say such blasphemous things!"

The two voices rang through the sacred cathedral. One was energetic, the other mean-spirited, and both were completely inappropriate to the setting. Hube didn't need to look to know who they belonged to. It was the redheaded hero, Arian, and her black-haired companion.

"Ha-ha-ha, maybe yours will get bigger if you prayed more passionately to the Goddess."

"…I've tried."

"Oops, my bad."

Arian looked down at her flat chest with a sullen face. Seeing this, the boy apologized in a serious tone and reached for her hand.

"Oh, don't be mad. I'll make you some pancakes as an apology," he said.

"Pancakes?! Those sweet and fluffy things? I love those!" replied Arian.

"Yeah? It'll have to be after we go to the market on the way back. I want to buy a pen and some parchments. Is that okay?"

"Yeah! But why do you need that? Have you been writing in a diary, too?"

"No, but I'm pretty confident in my drawing skills."

"You can draw?! Wow, okay, you have to draw me something later!"

"Okay. I'll draw you, all wet and sticky, getting attacked by the slime."

"Stop bringing that up already—!"

Arian turned bright red and playfully punched the boy's chest for teasing her.

As he watched the two warm up to each other, Hube's heart flared in a dark bitterness, unbefitting a man of faith.

"Bishop, is something wrong?"

"Nothing's wrong. Let us continue," replied Hube to the concerned priest, and he plastered a calm smile on his face before beginning to recite the prayer for the *Resurrection* spell.

Even though he knew he needed to concentrate in order to cast the spell, the reverberating voices tore at his heart.

"It really is a beautiful church… All right."

"Why do you touch the pillars every time we come to pray, Shinichi?"

"I'm actually super-interested in architecture, so I was trying to see how the church was built."

"I didn't know that! You're great with your hands, so I'm sure you'd make a wonderful craftsman."

"Do you have any dreams, Arian? It's not like you can be a hero forever."

"Uh, I haven't really thought about it…but I'd like to get married someday," admitted Arian flirtatiously. Her cheeks flushed in a deeper shade of red than her hair.

Her face held an expression of a maiden in love, which she'd never directed at Hube.

"…I apologize. It seems that I am a bit tired," said Hube, brushing away the confused priests as he bitterly cut off the spell.

He quickly returned to his room with hurried feet and cast a *Silence* spell to soundproof the walls before flinging off the books piled on his desk with all his strength.

"Those blasphemous bastards!" he screamed.

As the books hit the floor, they made a clamor, but the spell prevented this sound from leaking out of the room. As he continued pounding on his desk, he ground his teeth in an ugly, spiteful grimace, far from his public figure as the mild and moderate bishop.

"That lecherous servant of the Evil God coming to tempt and corrupt the Goddess's hero! *My* Arian!"

Knowing no one could hear him, he spit out every curse and damnation that came to mind. It wasn't necessary for him to name the target of his jealousy. It was the boy who'd suddenly come along and stolen Arian's heart.

It was the boy named Shinichi.

"She'll never go to defeat the Demon King if he leads her astray!"

If she didn't defeat the demons in Dog Valley soon, he'd not only fail to become archbishop, but his name would be tarnished. People would start doubting his faith, wondering whether he was just letting the enemies of the Goddess gallivant and roam around. The high-ranking officials of the church were ruthless in establishing their hierarchical order. It was hell: perpetually one-upping each other, tripping each other up, and dragging each other into a bottomless abyss if one wasn't careful enough.

"He must be eliminated."

He made his decision with his usual composure, calming down slightly. His only option was to take care of the boy for his sake—and for Arian's.

However, the silver-haired maid, who followed him around like a shadow, would be troublesome to deal with. He'd sent spies from the church to tail them, but the maid had put an *Enemy Sonar* spell and a *Hard Lock* spell on their rooms at the inn as a precaution, sealing them. There were no good opportunities for assassination.

And if he was to completely believe the spies' reports, the maid's magic was in the same league as his own, capable of *Full Healing* and even *Resurrection.* This meant he'd need to completely get rid of the boy's body for him to die. He could cut him up into little pieces with his sword and feed him to the fishes in the moat or use flames to incinerate him to his bones. In any case, it would draw too much attention and take too much time, and there was a chance Arian might see through his plans in the worst-case scenario.

"I suppose I could make the king work for me."

He could fabricate an appropriate crime that'd have the boy banished. Hube could probably pull something like that off, seeing as he pulled the strings of Boar Kingdom. But would Arian return to his side even if he was successful in executing this plan?

"Impossible! A hero would never stab a Goddess's bishop in the back..."

Hube reassured himself his quiet inner voice was just part of his imagination. He continued to agonize over the situation until the sun fell below the horizon line and night set in.

There was a knock at the door.

"Bishop Hube, do you have a moment?"

After knocking, a single priest opened the door and entered the room. He noticed the books scattered on the floor but didn't mention them, as he went to Hube's side to speak quietly into his ear.

"We've discovered something about the boy and his maid."

"What is it?"

As the bishop urged him to continue, the priest—a spy—was unusually nervous.

"Yes, um, right. The maid's a demon."

"...What did you just say?"

"The maid is a demon. I believe her companion is either a demon or a traitor to humankind."

"......"

Hube's mind blanked for a moment. As he stood there stunned, the spy continued his explanation with an expression that said he still wasn't sure if he believed it.

"There was a moment when the *Illusion* spell dissipated. She must have relaxed when they were alone."

When she did, her shining silver hair had stayed the same, but the color of her skin deepened, and her ears grew longer. She perfectly resembled a legendary dark elf, the fallen form of a forest fairy.

"They're also conspiring to ask 'the Demon King to prepare more gold' so they could try to 'curry favor from His Majesty again,' which leads us to believe we aren't mistaken."

"Ha...ha! Ha-ha-ha-ha!"

Finally comprehending the spy's report, Hube was unable to control his laughter.

"I thought he was an unholy heretic, attempting to lead the Goddess's hero astray, but to think he's an agent of the Evil God!"

He hated himself for being too foolish to see it sooner. At the same time, he thanked the Goddess from the bottom of his heart for giving him a reason to eliminate the boy.

There was one more truth that delighted him.

"He must also be the same merchant who disgraced me in front of the king. What a wonderful miscalculation on his part." He chuckled.

The merchant was the only figure who could talk of winning the king's support with gold. Thinking about it now, he realized that although the merchant's face had been hidden with grotesque burn scars, his height and build were the same as the boy's.

"Ah. This all makes sense. This is why I had a feeling of déjà vu when I saw the maid."

His silver-haired companion and the blue-haired maid at the audience chamber were surely the same person. Under a spell, her outer appearance was changed.

"If I had forced her to remove the *Illusion* spell right then and there, things would've been over much quicker. It seems I'm still lacking in diligence."

He'd noticed immediately that the maid was concealing her appearance with magic. But he didn't force her to reveal herself, because he was recovering from the shame of losing to the merchant—a sharp thorn that pierced his heart. This was quite the strategy if this was all part of his grand plan, revealing his burn marks to achieve this outcome.

But his little secret was out.

"Just as I thought. The Goddess would never turn a blind eye to evil," said Hube. He renewed his faith in the Goddess while planning to exterminate evil.

"Bishop, shall I immediately inform the king and ask the troops to be readied?" asked the spy.

The agents of the Demon King infiltrating the city was a serious issue. They should mobilize their entire army, surround them, and ensure they kill the agents in question.

Hube shook his head slowly at the spy's suggestion.

"No, that won't be necessary. Is there not someone more suited to eliminate these vile demons?" he prompted.

"That would be...," started the spy, trailing off when he realized whom Hube was speaking of.

"Would you be so kind as to bring this person to me?" ordered Hube, smiling as he patted the spy's shoulder.

The light that settled in his eyes was not that of a bishop executing the Goddess's will. It was the flames of dark envy of someone who desired a girl many times younger than him—the true and pathetic form of a middle-aged man.

"Ah, those pancakes were really tasty!"

In the afternoon, after they finished saying their prayers at church, Arian and Shinichi went shopping around town before he presented her with home-baked goods. Arian lay down on her bed at the inn, letting her cheeks widen into a smile.

"Shinichi really doesn't care about it, huh?"

On the night she revealed her true self as a half dragon, she'd prepared for the worst, but Shinichi's attitude toward her hadn't changed at all. In fact, it seemed like the distance between them had gotten shorter.

"And today, it kind of felt like we were on a date...," said Arian, her cheeks flushing red, even though she was the one who'd said it.

She'd been lonely when she ran from town to town with her mother and later became a monster hunter. She'd never had a male friend close in age, let alone a boyfriend, which made her all the more excited and bashful.

"Oh, a date... If we become boyfriend and girlfriend, I wonder if we'll kiss and stuff?" speculated Arian.

As she fantasized, she recalled the events of the other night in the back of her mind. She'd sadly lamented her fears, and he'd smiled at her wryly, as if to suggest he had no choice but to console her. Any normal person would've been grossed out, but he'd just calmly put his tongue on her—

"Aahhh! No, something was wrong with me that night!" Arian turned bright red at the memory, rolling around on the bed and trying to make up an excuse to no one in particular. "Ugh, seriously, why would I say something so embarrassing...?"

There'd come a time in the future when she'd be frozen with embarrassment when she discovered that male and female dragons twine together and lick each other's necks during courtship.

Right now, there was only one reason she was flustered.

"I think I like him..."

She had a lot of fun talking to Shinichi. When he suddenly got too close, her heart would start to race. When she saw him talking to Celes or other girls in the city, it felt like someone was squeezing her heart, a reaction so painful she wanted to cry.

She didn't have enough experience to know if this was love.

"I wonder how Shinichi feels about me."

He was always kind to her, so she didn't think he disliked her. But it felt like he wasn't being completely honest, though she couldn't say for sure. It felt like he was always guarded or wearing a mask.

Aside from the occasional teasing, he mostly smiled at her. But when he talked to Celes, he would get angry or wrinkle his eyebrows in annoyance. He showed a bunch of different emotions, but in the end, he looked happy and—

"—Ugh, no! I'm a hero of the Goddess! I shouldn't be thinking about things like that!" shouted Arian frantically to blow out the dark flames trying to take hold of her heart.

And then she remembered something.

Stricken by illness, her mom used to always say: "Arian, no matter how much pain you're in or how much it hurts, you should never hold a grudge."

There'd been times when she was unlucky, when someone saw the scales on her neck and called her a monster or threw stones at her.

But it was wrong to be angry. It was wrong to hate them. She had strength, the power of a dragon. Even if she followed her gut and killed someone, no one would've been able to punish her.

This was the reason why she needed to have self-control that was harder than steel.

Her mother had always assured her. "You're human. You're a bit stronger than other people, but you're human."

Yes, she was human, so she shouldn't kill other humans. She couldn't become one of the beasts that threatened humans—the monsters, demons, or even the dragons.

"Yeah, I know, Mom," said Arian, remembering her mother's words and steadying her heart.

She'd lived by those words: not hating anyone, smiling through the pain, and always fighting for others. It was this lifestyle that let her become a hero of the glorious Goddess, become friends with the people of this city, and find Shinichi, someone who understood and accepted her. It'd be ludicrous for a half dragon to ever hope for more happiness.

"Well, I'm allowed to like someone, right?" murmured Arian, like she was seeking forgiveness.

As if to answer her prayers, a knock came from the door.

"Ah?! O-one minute!"

Arian jumped from the bed in a fluster, patted her blushing cheeks, and tried to show a calm demeanor as she opened the door. But it wasn't the black-haired boy she kind of hoped it'd be but a priest clad in white robes.

"I'm very sorry to bother you late at night, but Bishop Hube requests your presence."

"The bishop?" asked Arian, cocking her neck in response to this unexpected demand.

That said, there's no way she could turn down a request from the person who'd saved her life and made her a hero. Arian put herself together and placed her new favorite sword, which she found together with Shinichi, at her hip. She headed toward the cathedral with the priest.

The inside of the cathedral was dimly lit, and the two walked down the aisle, eerily lined with corpses, before entering the prayer room in the back. In front of the giant statue of the Goddess, Bishop Hube stood in contemplative prayer. He turned to face them when he heard their footsteps, smiling.

"—gh!"

A shiver suddenly ran up Arian's spine when she saw his tranquil expression. It was somehow completely different from usual. Hube walked slowly up to Arian and spoke the following words.

"Hero Arian, as the bishop of our Goddess of Light Elazonia, I command you to eliminate the heretics, Shinichi and his attendant, from this world."

Kill the boy she loved with her own hands.

"Take extra care to completely destroy his body so he cannot stray into this world again."

"W-wait a minute!" yelled Arian, bewildered, at Bishop Hube, who smiled and spoke like he was apprehending a child for running and tripping. His composure opposed his command. "Why would you tell me to kill him?!"

"I already said why. He's a heretic and an agent of the demons."

"Th-there must be some mistake! There's no way Shinichi's working for the demons!"

"I understand why you might not want to believe it, but it's simply the truth," said Hube as he glanced at the priest who'd brought her. "You've surely noticed the boy's maid conceals her appearance using magic."

"I'm sure she has something she'd like to keep to herself…," said Arian. She herself had secret scales on her neck, so she did not push the matter any further. But—

"The maid's true form is a wicked demon, a dark elf."

"No, you're lying…"

"I speak only truth. Do you really think I'd deceive a hero, a devout follower of our Goddess, like you?" asked Hube. He spit out that final line, an obvious lie, clapping his hands on Arian's small shoulders.

"B-but I—," began Arian, desperately trying to resist, but the bishop bent down and whispered into her ear.

"You wouldn't want anyone to know who you truly are, would you?"

"—gh!"

Arian pulled back in shock, but Hube stared at the scarf and her concealed neck, as if to tell her she couldn't escape.

"H-how, bishop, do you—?!"

The only person in this country who should've known she was a half dragon was Shinichi.

"Our Goddess sees all" was all Hube said, conjuring up a fake smile at Arian, who was flustered and shaken with surprise.

It occurred to her the bishop might've succumbed to lust and used *Clairvoyance* to watch over women and children in private.

"All the people of this country rely on you. You know you can't let them down, right?"

This included the kind owner of the tavern and inn who treated her like she was a normal customer, like she was his own daughter. There were the easygoing guards at the gates who greeted her every morning as she went to train. There were the ladies, the children, the elderly, who all smiled when they saw her and thanked her for giving them another peaceful day.

She'd be hated by all of them if she were exposed as a tainted half dragon—a creature more hated and feared than the demons.

"I—I..."

Arian shook, her face pale with fear, and Hube gently patted her shoulders again.

"You'll see to it, right? Arian?"

Now that she was a hero, she'd finally found a sanctuary, a safe and welcoming place in reach. If it meant protecting that, there was only one answer she could give.

Arian returned to the inn, and dawn broke before she could rest her eyes.

Shinichi greeted her with his usual smile as she came down the stairs to the tavern with a horrible expression on her face.

"You look tired. You should eat something and rest," he said, offering her some candy.

Under normal circumstances, she would've happily thrown it in her mouth and chatted with him until the owner had finished making their breakfast. But those days were over now.

"Shinichi, let's go defeat the Demon King."

"...Okay." He misread her expression and assumed that it was from nerves and steadfast resolve. He nodded his head with a serious expression and went to his room to prepare for the journey in silence.

The owner watched with worried eyes as the three left the tavern.

"......"

Shinichi and Celes were unusually quiet on their walk northwest to Dog Valley, perhaps out of respect for Arian. She clung to that hope as she looked up at the clear sky, contrary to her clouded inner conscience, and just kept putting one foot in front of the other.

"Guess we'll rest here today," suggested Shinichi as the sky became a deep red, and the three of them stopped on a narrow forest path.

Arian watched him drop his pack and start preparing food before asking the question she'd been avoiding until now.

"Shinichi, it's a lie you're working for the demons, right?"

What are you talking about? Your food's going to get cold if you don't hurry.

This is what she wanted him to say with a smile like he always did, to laugh it off like he always did.

But she'd never seen him so serious. His expression betrayed any lingering hope.

"Celes," he said.

"Understood."

When she heard her name, Celes broke the spell that hid her form. Her long, plain skirt, her maid outfit, the figure Arian so envied, her facial features, and her silver hair did not change. But her skin darkened, and her ears grew threefold, ending in a sharp point.

"A dark elf..."

She was a demon, the Goddess's enemy, the Evil God's kin, one of the beasts who had killed three thousand of Boar Kingdom's soldiers.

She'd known and tried to prepare herself, but Arian was frozen by shock. Shinichi looked at her with serious eyes and confessed.

"As you can see, Celes is a demon and a loyal servant to the Blue Demon King. And I am human, but I serve the Demon King as his advisor."

As he spoke, he took an eerie smiling mask from his breast pocket and covered his face, as if to conceal his expression with it.

"Why? Why would you do this?!" Arian let out a heartrending shriek as she berated him. Shinichi removed the mask and threw it aside, telling her everything.

"I come from a different world, a world called Earth."

"Earth…?"

"And the Demon King summoned me to defeat the heroes who kept respawning to attack him."

"What are you saying?!"

"You don't have to believe me, but I'm the one who forced Ruzal and his companions to surrender and leave."

"What…?"

She didn't want to believe it.

She didn't want to believe he was working for the demons or the one who trapped the other heroes. She didn't want to believe everything he did was to bury all of them deep into the ground. Becoming her friend, lending her a hand, saying and acting like he didn't care that she was a half dragon, walking down the streets, making pancakes for her—all those nice memories were to consign her to oblivion. They were all lies. She didn't want to believe it.

"Liar! Please tell me that you're lying—!" pleaded Arian, sobbing, as she drew her sword and pointed it at Shinichi.

Celes immediately moved toward them when she saw this, but Shinichi stopped her with the motion of his hand.

"You decide what you believe," he said.

"What…?"

"There's no such thing as an absolute truth. There are unlimited truths of 'things that you want to believe.'" Shinichi wore a serious expression that belied no emotion. He waited for Arian's reply.

Do you believe all the Goddess's teachings are completely true and demons are an enemy that must be destroyed? Or will you work with them and make some interesting friends, even though they can be simpletons and come from a different culture than yours?

"What the hell? Don't try to deceive me with such ridiculous things!" screamed Arian furiously, but Shinichi's assertion did not change.

"I was summoned from a different world. I became the Demon King's advisor, and I defeated the heroes who were hostile toward the demons. That's it. The rest is up to you. You decide what happens next."

"That's so cowardly!"

She would have preferred for him to pathetically beg for his life. Then she would've been disillusioned, and she could cut him down without hesitation. Or she would've preferred if he'd just been kind and said it was all a misunderstanding and kept deceiving her. Then she could have forgotten everything and thrown herself into his arms.

But he told her the truth and left Arian to make the final decision. To kill him or to—

"You're a coward! A liar! Sick!"

"I didn't think you'd start saying that, too," said Shinichi. For the first time, his serious expression cracked with a small grin.

It was the same smile he'd always directed at her. It was a little troubled but kind.

"Ah, HYAAAAaaaa—!"

Arian's emotions burst inside her as she brandished her sword, lunging toward Shinichi, who kept smiling, making no attempt to dodge, and—

It was just past midnight. It wouldn't be long until the sun showed its face again. Arian walked down the dark aisle of the cathedral with a bowed head and leaden feet. The magic sword was missing from her side, and she was splattered with mud. Walking like a specter, she drifted unsteadily. She proceeded to the far back of the cathedral and opened the door to the prayer room.

Bishop Hube stood in front of the Goddess's statue in the unilluminated chamber, as if he knew she was about to return.

"Welcome back, Arian. Am I safe to assume the heretic has been eliminated?" he asked.

"...Yes."

Hube smiled gently and walked up to Arian. She nodded, as if she were about to crumble into pieces. He grasped her shoulders and let out a voice that could've come up from the bowels of hell.

"Heroes of the Goddess should not lie."

"—gh!"

Arian snapped her head up as if drawn by an invisible string, and at the same time, chains stretched up from the ground and wrapped around her body.

"Gah—!"

"So unfortunate. This is all so very unfortunate, Arian."

Following Hube's voice, more than thirty priests stepped out of the shadows, concentrating on the magic chains, as they slowly tightened their circle around her.

"I've already been informed that you let the heretics escape," said Hube. Behind him, the middle-aged priest who'd talked to her at the inn appeared.

He'd been sent to secretly follow her and make sure that she carried out the bishop's orders to lure Shinichi and Celes out of the city and kill them both.

"Why did you let the heretics go?" asked Hube. His expression was somehow gentle and ghastly at the same time. His gaze told her that he wouldn't accept any excuses. A single tear ran from Arian's eye.

"I couldn't carry out your orders to kill Shinichi!"

Heartbroken by his betrayal, she had pointed her sword at Shinichi, but in the end, she'd wavered. The sword had fallen from her hands, leaving him uninjured. Yes, he'd hidden from her that he was working for the demons, and yes, it'd all been part of a plan to bring down the heroes. But he was telling the truth when he said they'd become friends, that she was no longer alone, and that he didn't care she was a half dragon. When she listened to him and looked at his wry smile that accepted his inevitable death, she decided to believe him.

But that was just a pathetic attempt to circumvent the truth.

"I—I love Shinichi."

She liked him. She'd been swept away by love. This was why she believed him, forgave everything, overlooked everything, and ran away without asking any more questions.

The maid had been annoyed she was a dumbass girl to let herself be led on by a worthless boy like him.

"I love, I love him…!" repeated Arian. As she repeated this final phrase, her unrequited feelings stabbed her heart over and over again. They had failed to reach him. Large teardrops rolled down her cheeks.

Seeing the girl's tragic tears, the Goddess's Bishop Hube—

"Filthy traitor!" he screamed, bearing resemblance to a monster, as he slapped Arian's cheek with the flat of his palm.

"—gh!"

"Traitor! Apostate! To be defiled by an agent of a demon! You vile traitor!" he bellowed as he struck her face over and over. She didn't resist him, trapped more by her guilt than by the magical chains.

The surrounding priests were frozen in shock at the sight of his frenzied breakdown. They just stood there. None of them stepped forward to stop him.

"Do you know? How? Much? I've given you?"

He was the one who'd persuaded her to become a hero, even though she'd hesitated at first. He gave her every possible mission to defeat monsters so her name would be well-known throughout the kingdom. He'd kept the fact that she was a filthy half dragon locked away in his heart.

"Everything! Everything you have is because of me!"

Hube violently attacked Arian for her betrayal, dismissing the fact that everything he'd done had been for his own benefit, his advancement within the church. But it was less about choosing not to kill someone working for the demons. It was the betrayal of giving her heart to someone other than him.

"Huff, huff…"

Hube finally lowered his arm after striking her dozens of times. The bones in his hand hurt as if they'd been fractured.

Arian's cheek was swollen and bright red but quickly returned to normal. As a half dragon, her immense magical power gave her a sturdy corporeal body and faster regeneration than the average human. It meant that even the bishop, who specialized in healing spells, had no way to actually injure her.

Besides, she was a hero, a figure capable of resurrection. Between two heroes, killing each other was impossible.

But the Goddess's church had some precautions in place. After all, they'd relied on heroes for hundreds of years and learned some things along the way.

"It's so incredibly unfortunate I have to destroy an excellent hero like you," Hube said. He somehow managed to return his voice to normal, as he caught his breath and wrapped his hands around Arian's slender neck and scarf.

"—gh!"

"Prepare yourself. The torturers at the Holy See are truly brutal."

There was one way to render a hero powerless. Coincidentally, the Demon King's Dirty Advisor had also thought of it but never implemented it. This method was a product of a dark, mad mind.

"They'll place carnivorous insects in every orifice. You'll come to know the fear and pain of being eaten alive from inside out. The *Pain Block* spell won't help you. After they eat through a third of your brain, you'll be unable to maintain the spell, and in that moment, all your senses will return and overwhelm you."

"Hyagh—!" It was the ordinary priests who let out the shriek and started shaking after listening to his words, but Arian's expression didn't change. Her tears of repentance just kept running down her cheeks.

"I'm sorry..."

She spoke to the Goddess, who'd made her a hero and trusted her to look after the people, and to the bishop, who was the reason she'd become one.

And she spoke to her dead mother, who'd refused to abandon this half dragon and spent her life raising her.

"It's far too late for apologies!" Hube admired her for her dignity, for not groveling and begging for her life, even though she was afraid. His attraction to her lingered, which was why he raised his hand to strike her again.

But the blow didn't reach her face.

"That's enough domestic violence, bishop."

Hube didn't understand this phrase, but he could tell it was mocking him based on the voice's spiteful tone.

The speaker had just kicked open the doors to the prayer room, appearing before them with an exceptionally sinister smile. He'd loved watching every moment as they readily stumbled into his trap.

"Shinichi?!" Arian twisted around to see his face, and the black-haired heretic responded by sticking his thumb up.

"Sorry we're late. We're a bit busy carrying some corpses around," he said nonchalantly.

"I did most of the carrying," clarified Celes, seeming somewhat tired as she appeared behind him.

"What are you doing here?!" shouted Hube. His smile crumbled away, and he faltered.

Seeing this, Shinichi could not restrain his laughter.

"Hey, hey, did you really think we wouldn't notice Arian had been tailed?"

"I was the one who located him," Celes chimed in.

"By the way, we defeated all the guys you sent to finish us off. They're tied up, naked, in front of the city gates."

"I was the one who did that, too," she quickly added.

Celes was pretty burned out: She'd cast a *Fly* spell to go after Arian, who was running faster than a bullet train, and put a number of backup spells in place. Shinichi, on the other hand, seemed full of energy, beaming triumphantly as he happily explained his plan.

"It's amazing you moved into place exactly as I'd hoped. You didn't even realize I revealed my true form on purpose, ha-ha-ha!"

"You mean to tell me this was all part of your plan?!" cried Hube, refusing to believe him. To his surprise, Shinichi shook his head.

"No way. You can't really call this a strategy. It's more like a half-baked, haphazard gamble."

That's exactly what it was: a gamble in fate's hands. He had no control over its success or failure. This plan didn't rely on Shinichi's success. It banked on Hube's failure.

"I wanted to pull Arian over to the demon's side, but there was one massive obstacle... That obstacle was you, Bishop Hube," said Shinichi calmly.

"Me?"

"Yes, you're the person she owed for making her a hero and the person she respected like a father, in place of her dead mother."

"......"

Hube was silent. He couldn't express his genuine pleasure and joy. Shinichi's evil smile widened.

"And you're the one who ruined it all," said Shinichi.

Hube had been trapped by his bitter jealousy toward Shinichi and his desire to have Arian all to himself.

"You had so many opportunities to prevent this from happening."

He could've gone to kill Shinichi himself or sent the kingdom's military when he learned Shinichi was working for the demons. Instead, he made the twisted decision to have Arian do it with her own hands. Alternatively, he could've trusted Arian when she accepted his orders to eliminate them and not followed her. He could've shown compassion toward her broken heart and forgiven her for letting an enemy go. If only he'd shown some faith and leniency, this never would've happened.

"Put simply, your deviance welcomed this outcome," Shinichi summarized.

"Agh—!"

Happily ignoring his own shortcomings, Shinichi smiled his most ungodly smile and looked at the speechless Hube.

"Hey, how do you feel right now? How do you feel now that you've realized your lust for a younger girl and your jealousy destroyed everything you have?"

"You bastard—!" cried Hube. He was so furious, he didn't even realize the surrounding priests now knew his secret desire for Arian.

But he was able to push down his flaring rage and control his emotions, as he'd learned to do over the course of many years. He regained some semblance of composure.

"Ha… The runaway heretic just walked himself into the lion's den! This is also as the Goddess wills," said Hube.

This was his chance.

Even though the maid had an incredible capacity for magic, enough to fend off his assassins, she was likely so exhausted she only had one or two more spells in her. That detestable heretic boy knew some magic, but he'd be fighting alone. Compared to that, Hube's team was busy keeping Arian bound, but there were still over thirty of them. Even a child could see which side had the advantage.

"Everyone, we'll finish the traitor's punishment later. Right now, we must eliminate the heretic," ordered Hube, raising his hand toward Shinichi.

He might specialize in healing and resurrection spells, but he knew enough attack spells to kill someone. After all, he'd led his inferiors to defeat monsters as he worked his way up to bishop.

The threats seemed to have as little effect on Shinichi as water off a duck's back. He stared at the bound girl.

"Arian, I didn't have a chance to say this to you before. I'm working for the demons, but I have no desire to hurt people. Moreover, I want to ask you to end this pointless fighting between the humans and demons," said Shinichi.

"…What?"

"Making ties with the demons is a sinful act in and of itself," interjected Hube, but Shinichi paid him no mind.

"Arian, as you can see, I'm a dirty and lecherous asshole, and I played with your emotions. But even so, I think it'd be nice to work toward somewhere that's fun to be, where it doesn't matter if you're human or demon, if you have scales, if you believe in the Goddess or not, where you're not persecuted or killed for such stupid little things."

He didn't say he wanted the whole world to be fair and peaceful. He wasn't that much of a saint. But it was true he wanted those around him happy, even if that only extended to the people closest to him.

"Yeah, that's what I want to do. I want to make a fun country."

His own words finally made him realize this. He'd been going with the flow, moving forward without putting much thought into it. He'd been summoned by the Demon King, followed his instructions to defeat the undying heroes, gotten rid of a threat against his friends, infiltrated Boar Kingdom, and now he was here, witnessing Arian's capture. But he could finally see a goal at the end of the path he'd been walking. He placed a lot of importance on his own happiness, which was exactly why he wanted to make a place where the people around him could have fun and laugh.

This was the reason why Shinichi Sotoyama was in this world.

"So will you trust me? Will you put your life in my hands?" Shinichi asked, laughing and extending a hand toward Arian, who looked back in shock.

This was the boy who'd deceived her with kind words and come clean to her when he couldn't do it anymore. Now he'd come to save her.

If he promised to continue looking at her with this smile, she already had her answer.

"Yes. I give you my life, my heart, my everything," she said, stretching her bound hand as far as she could, asking that he take her with him.

Looking at the warm tears and gentle smile on Arian's face, Celes had only one thought: *...Oh man. She really is a dumbass.* But she was too bitter to say they suited each other.

"I'm tired of listening to all this talk. Now, begone!" said Hube. His anger was visible as he started to recite an incantation, but he was far too slow.

He'd lost the moment he stood in the center of the cathedral.

"*Fire!*" cried Shinichi, faster than Hube, who was unable to release his attack spell. Shinichi brought his right thumb down as if to press a switch.

In that moment, the dozens of thick pillars holding up the cathedral roared and exploded from the inside.

"Wh-what is this?!" screamed Hube, but there was no way he or the priests would know.

Every day, Shinichi had come to the cathedral and pretended to pray. He'd changed the material of the pillars little by little into nitroglycerin—the base ingredient of dynamite—using his *Element Conversion* spell, saturating the pillars so they would explode with the smallest flame.

"Ha-ha-ha, I bet you've always wanted to be killed by the Goddess's cathedral!"

"Let's leave," said Celes, grabbing Shinichi by his collar as he gloated and using her remaining magic to cast a *Fly* spell. With a backward glance at the trapped priests, they flew out of the collapsing church.

"Y-you heretic—!" screeched Hube. His last moments were filled with hatred as the giant Goddess statue toppled over, crushing him.

Under the warm light of daybreak, the ground rumbled, shook, and echoed as the Goddess's cathedral slowly imploded. Shocked residents woke from their slumber, while Shinichi, who'd escaped unharmed thanks to Celes, stared calmly at the magnificent scene.

"Man! It really is fun destroying something people put so much effort into making!" he said.

"That's the sickest, most twisted statement in all of history," Celes shot back, not forgetting to insult him as she collapsed onto the ground, exhausted.

Behind them, there was a mountainous pile of soldiers' dead bodies. It went without saying that Shinichi and Celes hadn't killed them. They were the soldiers whose hearts had been pierced by the Demon King. Celes and Shinichi had brought them out of the cathedral so they wouldn't be crushed. The soldiers had simply been doing their job when they'd attacked the demons, and the pair had no personal grudge against them. They couldn't bear to rob these soldiers of their chance at resurrection. As for the thirty or so priests who'd been buried by the cathedral… Well, let's just hope they all had the Goddess's protection or something.

"All right, let's get out of here before too many onlookers show up," said Shinichi. The rubble and debris started to settle, and knowing it was still dangerous, he cautiously stepped into the crumbled remnants of the cathedral. "Heeey! Arian, are you okay?"

In response to his call, a crumbled wall flew away from the rubble. Out of the debris, the dust-covered redhead jumped out.

"Pah… Shinichi, don't you think this was a little extreme?"

"Well, that's why I asked if you'd put your life in my hands."

Pouting, Arian came forward, not having sustained any serious injuries. Shinichi had destroyed the cathedral based on his belief that she'd be able to escape when the priests let go of their magical chains to save themselves.

"All right, let's go," said Shinichi.

He'd already turned his back to the humans. He was returning to the demon world.

One day, he was going to build a country where everyone—humans, demons, and half dragons—could live together happily.

Shinichi smiled at Arian and extended a hand toward—

"Force!"

He was flung back by an invisible blast of energy.

"Gah—!"

"Shinichi?!" screeched Arian, racing toward him as he coughed up blood.

As if to block her, a man crawled out of the debris between them.

"H-huff… You heretic, did you really think you could escape that easily…?" asked Hube. His eyes were bloodshot, and he looked at them with a crazed smile on his pale face.

There wasn't a single injury on his body.

"Tch, oh yeah, he's a hero, too…," remarked Shinichi, choking on his blood and clicking his tongue in annoyance at his own carelessness.

Hube had been crushed and killed by the Goddess's statue, but he'd resurrected immediately through her power. He was exhausted, so he'd hidden his body in the rubble to recover and waited for his opportunity to strike back.

"Die, you bastard heretic—!" screeched Hube, completely consumed by hatred as he shot the finishing blow.

However, this invisible burst of energy never struck the Demon King's advisor. Faster than an arrow, Arian sprinted around Hube and threw herself in front of Shinichi like a shield.

"Arian?!"

"Shinichi, are you okay?" she asked.

"Idiot! I should be the one asking that!" said Shinichi, standing through sheer force of will and wiping away a single line of blood running from Arian's mouth with his finger.

"You saved my life, but girls shouldn't do such reckless things," he said.

"Ha-ha-ha, that's the first time you've gotten mad at me," replied Arian with a chuckle.

"Why are you happy? Are you a masochist?!" exclaimed Shinichi, finally making an unrestrained jab at her, as he'd previously only done with Celes.

Arian laughed loudly in relief before turning to the bishop. He was rigid in shock for hurting her, but it was far too late.

She bowed her head deeply.

"I'm so grateful you made me a hero and always looked out for me," she said. Her smile didn't hold any resentment or anger. It only showed gratitude and sorrow for parting ways, as a bride might feel toward her father on her wedding day.

"A-Arian...," stammered Hube, pierced by Arian's clear and honest gaze. It was the reason he'd lusted after her for so long. All his rage and strength drained from his body, and he fell to his knees in the rubble.

"Good-bye, bishop," said Arian, turning her back to him and lending her shoulder to Shinichi as they walked away.

"Please wait! Don't go...Ariaaaan—!"

No matter how loud he screamed, Arian would never look back.

Shinichi, Arian, and Celes walked over the rubble, past the remains of the cathedral. Celes lightly healed their wounds by using the small amount of magic she'd regained once they were far from the wreckage.

They slipped quietly through the shocked crowds of people gathering to see the aftermath of the cathedral's collapse, and they left the city.

"Is it okay to leave everything like that?" asked Celes. Her hood was pulled down low to cover her long ears as she gestured toward the cathedral behind them.

She was concerned that, if they left the bishop, he'd come after them for revenge, but Shinichi just brushed off her concerns with a smile.

"Don't worry about him. That's why I had the backup plan, right?"

"Yes, but will it actually be effective?" asked Celes. It wasn't that she doubted Shinichi. It was just that she was completely unfamiliar with human culture.

"Hey, what'd you do?" butted in Arian, puffing her cheeks out in annoyance at being the only one not in on the plan. Shinichi replied with his usual devious smile.

"We have this wonderful saying where I'm from: 'The pen is mightier than the sword.'"

"Huh?"

"You'll see. You'll understand soon, ha-ha-ha."

Arian only had one reaction to seeing Shinichi's wicked smile.

"That evil smile of yours… I think it's kind of hot," she said.

It went without saying Celes let out a heavy sigh, thinking this dumbass was a lost cause.

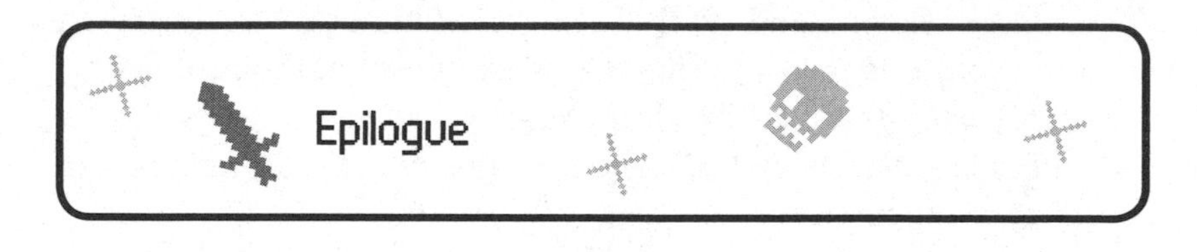

Hube crawled out from the ruins of the cathedral, waving away the gaze of curious onlookers with his hand, and hurried into the king's castle.

"At least I can get him!" he growled.

He knew the girl he so wanted would never return.

But at the very least, he wouldn't rest until he'd inflicted a horrifying death on that despicable usurper. As he pushed open the door to the audience chamber, the black desire for revenge was the only thing in his heart.

It was still early for the royal business to begin for the day, but everyone had woken up to the sounds of the cathedral collapsing. The king and all the lords who acted as his ministers were already present.

"Your Highness, we have a crisis!" said Hube.

"Hmm, a crisis indeed," replied King Tortoise IV dryly, in contrast to Hube's attempt to play up the tragedy to its utmost.

His face showed no bewilderment or fear despite the sudden destruction of the Goddess's cathedral. It almost seemed like he already knew the entire situation.

"Your Highness...?" began Hube.

"Well then, bishop," said the king, gesturing toward a minister, who walked up to Hube. In the minister's hand was a sheet of parchment.

"Do you have any justification for your crimes?" asked the king.

"...What?" Hube stood stupidly, completely unable to understand what the king was talking about. He looked down at the paper in his hands. He was lost for words when he saw what was written on it.

Sex abuse in the church! Bishop uses position of authority for repeated sexual harassment of hero!

And beneath it, there was an oddly well-drawn image of him with a lewd face, tearing the clothing off Arian, who was refusing his advances.

It went on to say the Goddess destroyed the cathedral as divine punishment for the bishop's wicked deeds.

"Wh-what is this?" he stammered.

"I'd hoped to ask the same thing," replied the king. His eyes were frosted cold as he gazed upon the bishop and his flustered state.

When the king had heard the sounds of the cathedral collapsing, he'd sent out soldiers to investigate, and they'd all returned carrying these leaflets. They were scattered in the castle gardens and throughout the city.

"According to these papers, you, the bishop, raped the hero Arian, and the cathedral was destroyed as a result of your sins. On top of that, Arian fled Boar Kingdom, unable to endure what you put her through."

"Your Highness, you cannot possibly believe such absurd claims!"

"Well, do you have another explanation?"

"That... Arian betrayed us!" shouted Hube in response to the questioning. "The black-haired boy pretended to be her friend but was really an agent of the demons! He led Arian astray so she'd betray us, and he attacked the cathedral!"

Hube explained he'd attempted in vain to fight back against the boy. There were some lies and exaggerations mixed in, but overall, Hube told the truth. He spoke in a way that showed how mortified he was.

However, the cold gaze of the king and his ministers showed that Hube failed to stir the same emotions in them.

"What an interesting story. What proof do you have to show us?" asked the king coldly.

"The proof is..."

There was no proof. Everyone who could have testified on his behalf was buried beneath the rubble of the cathedral. Not only that, but they were all priests of Hube's church, meaning most people would think they were simply lying to cover for their bishop.

"I've only spoken with Arian a handful of times, and she's not only an excellent hero but also conscientious and polite. Even if we assume she was raped, she's not the kind of person who'd commit the great sin of destroying a Goddess's cathedral."

"......"

"Furthermore, I unfortunately haven't met this black-haired boy, but what makes you so sure he's an agent working for the demons? According to rumors among my soldiers, he helped Arian obtain a powerful magical sword that could defeat the Demon King."

"That was surely a ploy to get in her good graces! Oh yes, I almost forgot! He was also that heretic merchant with the vile plan of opening trade with the demons! He's truly a strategist to be feared!"

"That merchant? Ha-ha-ha! This is quite amusing," said Tortoise IV with a chortle to mock Hube for continuing to spit out these absurd lies.

It wasn't surprising they didn't believe him. They didn't know the truth, and Hube had no proof.

"Bishop, I considered being lenient and forgiving your crimes if you admitted them. This is quite unfortunate."

"Your Highness, you'd believe this absurd scrap of paper over my word?!" demanded Hube. But he realized something.

The king and the ministers hadn't taken this scandalous message as absolute truth. They believed it because they wanted to believe it. They finally had the justification needed to rid themselves of the arrogant, high-and-mighty bishop who'd always looked down on them. Even if they'd known the truth, their decision likely wouldn't have changed.

"Bishop Hube, based on these events, I'm forced to report this to the Holy See," said the king, issuing the closest thing to a death sentence with his limited power under the Goddess's church and his weakhearted nature.

A cathedral of the church had been destroyed, and a promising hero chased away. Hube was as good as dead once word of his immense failures reached the church. He'd either be posted in some backwater village or imprisoned for life deep within the cathedral. Regardless, there was no way he could ever hope to see the sun again, let alone advance to archbishop.

"That… Ridiculous…"

Even though he was a bishop and a hero, there was no way he could change the flow of events now. If he announced Arian was actually a half dragon, they'd just decide he was lying again.

Everyone in the audience chamber almost screamed in relief as they watched Hube collapse to his knees.

The pedophile bishop's despair is sure to make my dinner taste better!

Well, they weren't quite so sick or boorish, but they must have felt something similar as triumphant smiles spread across their faces.

"Aah, that's what you did?!" squealed Arian after Shinichi filled her in on his "Fabricated Scandal" strategy as they walked to the Demon King's castle.

"I thought if I destroyed his reputation, he'd stop his attacks on the demons, even on the off chance I failed to persuade you. Pretty effective, right?" asked Shinichi.

"Uh-huh, you're diabolic, Shinichi…," said Arian, her face pale, as she imagined the uproar in Boar Kingdom. "I wonder if the bishop is okay…"

Shinichi cracked a small grin at her kindness. She was still worried about Hube after all he'd put her through and in the wake of cutting ties with him.

"Hey, you can see the Demon King's castle from here," he said.

"Y-yeah…," murmured Arian.

The tall and secure walls of the Demon King's castle stuck out from the wild untamed land in Dog Valley. Arian was incredibly nervous as Shinichi took her hand and led her inside the castle. She had the Twisted

Advisor to vouch for her, but she had been their enemy at one point, fighting against them as a hero. It wouldn't be surprising if they killed her.

Arian readied herself for the possibility, but the actual reaction from the demons was the complete opposite.

"Welcome, little Miss Hero!"

"Nice to meet you, Ms. Arian. Shinichi's told us all about you. Yes, ma'am!"

When the castle gates opened, the Demon King and Rino were there, awaiting their arrival with warm smiles.

"This is the kid who hurt the King, *oink*? Small but impressive, *oink*."

"I guess humans aren't too bad, *moo*."

"I hope we'll get to know each other!"

The other demons were waiting, too, eyes filled with curiosity, as they crowded around Arian to welcome her. No one held it against her that she was both a human and the hero who'd fought against them. They respected her strength and seemed happy to have a new friend.

"Uh, um? But I...," started Arian, confused by their reactions.

"Don't worry. Everyone in this castle is like this." Shinichi patted her shoulder reassuringly.

Of course, not all demons were this warm and welcoming. This crowd had been specifically chosen to enter the human world because their personalities were gentle and they wouldn't wreak havoc on humankind. She was still surprised there didn't seem to be any hatred in their eyes toward a human like her. There was only one thing they used to measure a person—strength.

"Oh, and by the way, here!" said Shinichi as he stole Arian's scarf from her neck.

"Ah!" shrieked Arian, panicking and covering her neck with her hands. But it was too late. The crowd had already gotten a good look at the red, glittering scales on her throat, and this image was burned into their minds.

"Ooh, so you really are a half dragon."

"Wow, the scales are so pretty! They're like little gems!"

"Since they're red, does that mean you're the child of the Red Dragon, *oink*?"

"I wonder which is stronger: the Red Dragon in the human world or the Black Dragon in the demon world, *moo*!"

The demons were surprised at this rare sight, but everything they said was positive. In fact, they neither regarded her in fear nor spewed hatred or ridicule.

"Um, why…?" began Arian.

"This is just the way they are," said Shinichi.

Although humans viewed scales as a symbol of a heretic, if the extent of one's disfigurement was just a few scales on the neck, the demons viewed it as a unique physical feature. After all, they were used to seeing snake women and merpeople.

"Are you glad you came?" asked Shinichi.

She spent a second to bask in this moment before answering his question with a nod and a brilliant smile.

"…Yeah!" said Arian.

"Shinichi, we've cleared up some of our busy work, but you must know this isn't the end," said the King, switching topics as the introductions began dying down.

"I am well aware, Your Highness," replied Shinichi, deeply nodding his head.

Boar Kingdom had lost their strongest hero and Bishop Hube his power and position. They probably wouldn't attack the demons any time soon. Considering Tortoise IV's personality, it's possible nothing else would ever come from them.

But that didn't mean the Goddess's church was just going to let them be. They had an abnormally staunch belief that demons were their mortal enemies, who they must attack and eliminate by any means necessary. This was all done in order to uphold the Goddess's teachings, the pillar of their faith. Backed by faith and their control over the *Resurrection* spell, they'd continue to find new heroes and enjoy authority over the people. There was no fear in Shinichi's heart, even though he knew they might face zealots from the church.

"No matter what hardships we encounter, I'll carve a path forward with my wisdom," asserted Shinichi with dramatic flair as he put on his mask again.

After all, he'd made a promise to Arian. He'd promised her they'd build a country full of joy, somewhere where people weren't persecuted over stupid little things, a place where everyone could laugh and have a good time.

That's why Shinichi had been brought to this world: to be the brain for these strong, fun, stupid demons and use any cowardly or twisted means required.

"Hmph, in that case. Shinichi, I, Ludabite Krolow Semah, the Blue Demon King, command thee," decreed the Demon King, picking up on his advisor's change of heart, "to give my beloved daughter, Rino, all the yummiest food in the human world!"

"Didn't I tell you to be cool?!" shouted Shinichi. It always came down to this! His final retort echoed throughout every nook and cranny of the castle.

This was the boy who'd be called the greatest traitor of the human race in history books for centuries to come.

This was how his story began.

Afterword

Hello, Famitsu Bunko readers. Sakuma Sasaki here.

First of all, I'd like to thank everyone for picking up this book.

As you might have guessed from the subtitle, this story was born from the idea of a world where the heroes never die, like in *D—gon Quest*, the crowning jewel among Japanese role-playing games (RPGs). In the game, a player can respawn after losing a battle by giving up half of their cash on hand. The creators of the game were probably thinking this would be the saving grace of Japanese gamers, who weren't really used to RPGs on their computers at the time. But if you think about it from the perspective of the Demon King, this is a truly horrific situation.

The heroes would resurrect no matter what he did, which meant there was no way he could defeat them. Moreover, he was in a position where he'd definitely be killed at some point… The word *cheat* hadn't yet been defined at the time, but I bet the Demon King would've complained, "They're cheating! This game is hella rigged!"

The only way this pitiful Demon King could stay alive is if he somehow got the player to stop playing. He could bore the players by setting up encounters with some small monsters every three steps to stall them. Or he could secretly place items needed to progress the story on random roadsides with no hints to their locations. Or he could fill the story with stupid and tedious characters to drain the player's spirit and morale to continue reading game exposition. He could use other tactics to put the player under a lot of stress until they exclaimed, "I'm through with this stupid game!" and indefinitely put gameplay on hold.

The Demon King wins the game when the players give up.

"In other words, all those shitty games were really just the stories where the boss won beat the players!"

"Wait, whaaaaaat—?!"

I'm obviously just joking.

But it's true that when you can't physically defeat an enemy, you're only left with psychological attacks to force them into submission. That's how this book was born—to protect the Demon King by breaking the heroes' psyches.

To cause someone to have a mental breakdown, the main character naturally had to have a particularly sick and twisted personality. I think there may have been some unpleasant scenes, but I hope you were able to enjoy the book, even if it was just a little bit.

Lastly, I would like to thank the incredibly talented Asagi Tosaka, who breathed life into my characters through her illustrations, my editor Kimiko Bugi, who was always so polite during our interactions, all the people at the printer, and anyone else involved in the publication of the book. Most of all, I'd like conclude this book by thanking my readers for picking it up and giving it a try.

Sakuma Sasaki, January 2017

P.S. All the heroines in this novel are older than ten, but only one is older than eighteen.

Afterword
Nice to meet you. My name is Asagi Tosaka. I really enjoyed reading about Shinichi's strategies for beating the Goddess's heroes, which were just as dirty as the title claims. I'm pretty sure I wouldn't have been able to handle going through all that (lol). On top of it all, the girls in the story were just so cute...!
I don't have too much experience designing characters with strong fantasy elements, so it took some time to mull over their designs. I'd like to keep trying!
Well, thank you for reading until the very end. Until we meet again!
遠坂あさぎ
Asagi Tosaka

The DIRTY WAY to DESTROY the GODDESS'S HEROES
Damn You, Heroes! Why Won't You Die?

"At your command, even if it takes my life!"
Arian
A bright and cheerful young hero with a brave and humble heart. She's considered the kingdom's rising star and is widely known for single-handedly defeating a massive black wolf.
"What do you think you're doing? Do you intend to grope my ass and use that memory to pleasure yourself later? Disgusting."
Celes
A maid who is always at the Blue Demon King's side. She is assigned to support Shinichi in battle. She's a powerful magic user, second only to the Blue Demon King himself. Though she rarely shows her emotions, she has a mercilessly sharp tongue.

"With these hands, I will definitely defeat these death-defying 'heroes.'"
"It was just so delicious..."
Rino
The daughter of the Blue Demon King, bestowed with an unusually lovely appearance and kind personality—for a demon. She ate bread from the human world, which catalyzed her desire to consume all sorts of delicious dishes.
Shinichi Sotoyama
An abnormally brave high school student summoned by the Blue Demon King to beat back the heroes. He accepts the King's command, figuring he might as well take advantage of being in another world.

"Shinichi..."
When she said his name, her voice was sweeter than the candy he'd conjured with magic.
As Arian looked at Shinichi with dewy eyes, her cheeks were flushed, and she breathed heavily. There was no trace of a little girl and her usual childish enthusiasm. In its place, there was the face of a passionate young woman.